Fear

13 STORIES OF
SUSPENSE AND HORROR

FEAR

13 STORIES OF SUSPENSE AND HORROR

· EDITED BY ·

R.L. STINE

DUTTON CHILDREN'S BOOKS

An imprint of Penguin Group (USA) Inc.

DUTTON CHILDREN'S BOOKS
A division of Penguin Young Readers Group

═══════════════ PUBLISHED BY THE PENGUIN GROUP ═══════════════

Penguin Group (USA) Inc., 375 Hudson Street, New York, New York 10014, U.S.A. ▼ Penguin Group (Canada), 90 Eglinton Avenue East, Suite 700, Toronto, Ontario, Canada M4P 2Y3 (a division of Pearson Penguin Canada Inc.) ▼ Penguin Books Ltd, 80 Strand, London WC2R 0RL, England ▼ Penguin Ireland, 25 St Stephen's Green, Dublin 2, Ireland (a division of Penguin Books Ltd) ▼ Penguin Group (Australia), 250 Camberwell Road, Camberwell, Victoria 3124, Australia (a division of Pearson Australia Group Pty Ltd) ▼ Penguin Books India Pvt Ltd, 11 Community Centre, Panchsheel Park, New Delhi—110 017, India ▼ Penguin Group (NZ), 67 Apollo Drive, Rosedale, North Shore 0632, New Zealand (a division of Pearson New Zealand Ltd.) ▼ Penguin Books (South Africa) (Pty) Ltd, 24 Sturdee Avenue, Rosebank, Johannesburg 2196, South Africa ▼ Penguin Books Ltd, Registered Offices: 80 Strand, London WC2R 0RL, England

This book is a work of fiction. Names, characters, places, and incidents are either the product of the author's imagination or are used fictitiously, and any resemblance to actual persons, living or dead, business establishments, events, or locales is entirely coincidental.

CIP Data is available.

Published in the United States by Dutton Children's Books,
a division of Penguin Young Readers Group
345 Hudson Street, New York, New York 10014
www.penguin.com/youngreaders

Designed by Jason Henry

Printed in USA ▼ First Edition
ISBN 978-0-525-42168-9
3 5 7 9 10 2 6 4 2

INTRODUCTION

· R.L. STINE ·

"AAAAAAAGGGGGGGGGGHHHH!"

I know you couldn't really hear that—but I wanted to start this book with a scream of horror.

That's just the first scream. Don't worry—there will be plenty more. And don't be surprised if *you* are the one doing the screaming!

I love stories with thrills and chills, shocks and twists, and horrifying surprises. If you have opened this book and are reading this introduction, you probably like them, too.

The people at ITW, the International Thriller Writers, asked me to fill a book with heart-pounding adventures and creepy-crawly mysteries, and I found thirteen stories that fill the bill. Lucky thirteen, right?

Well, you'll be lucky if you can make it through these

stories without shakes and shudders, chattering teeth, and chills running up and down your back.

Take, for example, Ryan Brown's story, "Jeepers Peepers." Elizabeth thinks she's going on a normal babysitting job. But why does the baby have to live in total darkness? And why does he keep warning her about mind creepers?

Or, how about Meg Cabot's fast-paced thriller, "The Night Hunter"? Nina has a boring job at the mall—until she sees a bank being robbed. She should have stayed away, but now she finds herself at the mercy of a mysterious young man known as the Night Hunter.

One of my favorites is "The Perfects" by Jennifer Allison. This story grabbed me with its amazing first sentence:

"The chances are pretty good that I'm going to be killed before daylight, and I can't help but think this never would have happened if we hadn't moved to Entrails, Michigan."

Wow. That made me keep on reading!

Heather Graham provides a chilling Halloween story, "She's Different Tonight." Of course, it involves a cemetery late at night. I don't want to give anything away. But there might be a vampire or two lurking among the tombstones.

And wait till you meet Soo-ling Choi in James Rollins's thrill-a-minute story, "Tagger." Soo-ling keeps picturing a disaster that destroys her whole city. Can the mysterious Chinese symbols she paints defeat her horrifying visions?

I'm not telling.

And I'm not going to give away any more secrets of our thirteen stories. Lots of thrills and chills await you. I think you should start reading.

And screaming . . .

CONTENTS

Fear

13 STORIES OF
SUSPENSE AND HORROR

WELCOME
TO THE CLUB

· R.L. STINE ·

JJ stepped back from the steamy dishwasher, eyes burning. He used his stained apron to wipe sweat off his forehead. His short, black hair felt wet, as if he'd just stepped from a hot shower.

He pulled the apron over his head, tossed down the dish towel, dried his hands on the legs of his jeans, and started to the open kitchen door. "Taking a five-minute break."

Florian turned and gave him the fish-eye. "Didn't you just take a five-minute break?"

"Yeah. Last night," JJ said.

"Make sure it's only five minutes." Florian raised a

hairy arm and made a show of checking his watch. He shook his head and slapped his metal spatula on the fry grill.

JJ stepped out onto the gravel parking lot and sucked in a deep breath of cool night air. The air made his hot face tingle. "I hate this restaurant."

Well, he didn't hate the restaurant. JJ wasn't afraid of work. He'd had jobs since he was twelve, five years now. He hated Florian, the fat hairball manager. Hated his blobby face, his stringy brown hair, his pig-snout nose, his fat mouth with the brown mole poking off one lip.

JJ had known guys like Florian back in Texas. Losers who tried to be big by pushing other losers around. Tough guys always on your case, trying to make you feel smaller than you were.

"All hat and no cattle." That's what they called blowhards like Florian in Texas.

Well, I'm not a loser, JJ thought. But I need this crummy busboy job. Mom is working two jobs, and we're just barely getting by. Only time I see her is when she's coming in from one job or heading out to the other. Guess I can put up with Florian for a while. At least he pays in cash.

JJ heard a girl laugh. He raised his eyes to the back

of the dark parking lot. Those kids from his school were back there again, sitting on the fenders of an old Pontiac GTO, smoking and giggling and goofing around.

That seemed to be their nightly hangout. JJ knew they could see him in the light from the open doorway. But they ignored him. They ignored him in school, too, which maybe was a break. At least they weren't smirking at his Texas accent or making fun of his hand-me-down flannel shirts and raggedy jeans.

JJ had been the new kid in school lots of times, and it was never a picnic. First time up north, though, and being ignored was definitely a relief.

He was good-looking enough—the dark, serious features he inherited from his dad, and the tall, lanky grace he got from his mom. But Fremont High was big— bigger than some of the towns he'd lived in. And so far, no one had looked at him twice.

A break. JJ hadn't had too many breaks in his seventeen years. His dad lost job after job, moved the three of them from hick town to hick town. Then last fall, he moved them up north—and got himself killed in a stupid truck accident.

Once JJ got over the shock, he decided it was just one more move in his life, one more fresh start. *I just got to stay out of trouble*. Yes, there'd been some trouble back in Texas. Some suspended-from-school-type trouble. And some bad trouble.

But who could blame him?

Behind him, JJ could hear Florian screaming at Julie, the only waitress. "You weren't born that ugly. You had to grow into it!"

Julie isn't ugly, JJ thought. She was plain. But Florian kept insisting if she did herself up nicer, she'd get bigger tips. JJ and Julie both knew that Florian cheated her out of most of her tip money, anyway.

"Go ahead. Drop another glass!" Florian was shouting. "I'll take a dozen glasses out of your pay! And don't backtalk me, girl. Think I don't know who eats all the breakfast Danish? Think that isn't stealing?"

He liked to make Julie go all pale and start her chin quivering. Too bad she really needed her job.

JJ let out a long sigh. He kicked the gravel with his boot, turned, and slumped back into the steamy kitchen.

"Where you been? On vacation?" Florian snapped. "Think I pay for your vacations? Don't give me no looks, punk. I'll smack you down. No lie!"

A little before closing time, the kids from the back of the parking lot came ambling into the restaurant. JJ was stacking plates under the counter. He watched them push each other into the blue vinyl booth at the far corner.

He recognized the girl. Maria Valdez. He noticed her at school. She was sexy and dark, with straight black hair and lots of black eye makeup—black fingernails, too. Not a goth. Just trying to be interesting, he guessed. And she was.

He also recognized the dude everyone called Bony. He was good-looking in a tough kind of way—long, wavy hair; a tight smile; steely gray eyes, cold eyes; and a tiny stud in one ear. He dressed tough, too, in black T-shirts with heavy-metal-band logos and straight-legged black denims, a frayed leather jacket with the word KILLERS in red across the back.

JJ saw two other guys he didn't recognize. One of them had his face in a portable game player and was thumbing frantically. The other guy was big, like a football linebacker. He had a Red Sox cap pulled down over his forehead. He was holding the plastic menu upside down, pretending to read it.

JJ grabbed a handful of silverware and started to their table. "Hi." Maria greeted him with a smile. The others turned to stare at him. "We've seen you in school, right?"

"He's the new kid," the big dude said.

JJ nodded. "Yeah. I'm the new guy. JJ."

Bony narrowed his eyes at him. "JJ? Does that stand for anything?"

"No," JJ replied. "Just initials. It's a Texas thing."

Maria leaned close and raised her dark eyes to him. "Can you get us free Cokes?" she whispered.

He wasn't sure he heard her. "Excuse me?"

"Come on, man," Bony said. "No one's watching. Free Cokes. You can do it, right?"

"No," JJ said. He turned to see where Florian was. Probably in back. "I don't think so. I need to keep this job. I—"

Maria put her hand on his. She had a very sexy smile. "You can do it, JJ. . . . It's just Cokes."

"Julie, get your butt over to that table!" Florian's shout made JJ jump.

"Why is the idiot busboy talking to the customers?" Florian yelled. He slapped his fat hands on the counter. "JJ, get back to the kitchen with the other cockroaches!"

JJ could feel his face grow hot. He knew he was blushing. Maria laughed. She squeezed his hand. JJ dropped the silverware on the table and hurried to the kitchen. "Sorry, sir. Sorry."

A few minutes later, he saw Florian go down to the cellar to deal with the garbage. JJ waited a short while to make sure he wasn't coming right back up. Then he strode to the soda dispenser and poured four Cokes for Maria and her friends.

Julie saw what he was doing, but she didn't care. She helped him punch the right keys on the cash register to make it look like the kids had paid.

Bony flashed him a thumbs-up. The other two guys grinned at him. "You're okay, dude. Be true to your school, right?" That made them all laugh.

He could hear Florian lumbering up the stairs. JJ hurried back to the dishwasher. Why did he give them free Cokes? To put it to Florian. And well . . . maybe he was tired of being ignored. All those hours in school, silent, with no one to talk to. Maybe he needed a few friends.

Especially Maria?

Florian burst into the kitchen and gave JJ a shove. "Hey, worthless, didn't you hear me calling you to come down and help?"

"Sorry, sir," JJ replied with his best Texan politeness. "Please don't shove me, sir."

"Shove you? I'll smack you upside the head!" the fat blob shouted. "What are you going to do, sue me?"

After work, Maria, Bony, and the other two guys were still at the back of the parking lot. JJ stretched his arms above his head, shook off the steamy air of the kitchen that clung to his skin, his clothes. He headed to their car, his boots kicking up gravel as he walked.

Maria sat on the half-rusted hood of the GTO. Bony had an arm around her waist. The other two leaned on the side of the car.

"Thanks for the free drinks, man," Bony said. He reached his free hand out, and he and JJ touched knuckles.

"No problem," JJ muttered. He had his eyes on Maria, and she knew it. Her dark eyes flashed.

"That's Sammy and Eduardo." Bony pointed to the other two guys. "They don't go to school anymore."

"What do you guys do?" JJ asked.

Eduardo shrugged. "Whatever we can get away with."

All four of them laughed. JJ thought about laughing, but it was too late. Maria had a great laugh, he decided. Very open. He liked the way she tossed back her head when she laughed, and her hair swung back on her shoulders.

"Well, thanks again, man," Bony said, patting JJ's shoulder, like he was a dog. "We could pay for the Cokes, you know. We were just kinda testing you."

JJ took a step back. "Testing me?"

Bony nodded. "You know. See if you had any guts."

JJ felt his jaw clench. "I've got guts," he said, staring Bony in the eyes.

"Well, we like to test people," Bony said, squeezing Maria's waist. "In case they want to hang with us."

"It takes a special dude," Sammy said. He had a strange, scratchy voice, like a cartoon character. "It's a club, you know."

JJ shook his head. A breeze fluttered his flannel shirt. It brought a chill to the back of his neck. "A club?"

The three guys nodded. They had strange smiles on their faces. But their eyes were serious. "The Killers," Maria said. "That's us." Bony turned and showed off the word KILLERS embroidered on the back of his leather jacket.

Bony hardened his stare. *Like he's trying to invade my brain or something*, JJ thought.

"If you want to join our club, there's an initiation," Bony said softly.

JJ looked away. "Like what?"

Bony didn't have a chance to answer. The kitchen door of the restaurant swung open, sending a flood of light over the parking lot. "You punks better get outta here!" Florian screamed. He filled the doorway, blocking most of the light. JJ saw he was swinging a butcher knife. "I already called the cops. You jerks got maybe a *minute* to scram outta my parking lot!"

JJ ducked behind the side of the car. Did Florian see him? He didn't want to lose his job because of these guys. They were scrambling into the car. A hand grabbed JJ's. Maria. She pulled him into the backseat.

The car squealed away, shooting up a shower of gravel. JJ pressed against Maria and ducked his head. He glimpsed Florian's angry scowl and the big blade of the knife swinging in front of him.

They roared through town, laughing like lunatics. JJ laughed, too. Something broke free in him. For a while, he thought he was flying. Maria's hair brushed his face. She smelled like flowers.

They stopped in Fremont Park, across from the high school. Bony killed the engine and the lights. They dove out of the car and sprawled in the dew-wet grass. They were all breathless and giddy.

"It's a club, see," Bony said, as if they hadn't been interrupted. "But I don't know if you're man enough for the initiation."

JJ gulped in the cool, fresh air. "Try me."

"The name says it," Eduardo told him. He pounded the back of Bony's jacket. "KILLERS, see?"

"I don't see," JJ said.

"That's the initiation," Maria whispered. Her breath tickled his ear. Was she coming on to him?

"Guess I have to spell it out," Bony said. He tore up a handful of grass and let it sprinkle over Maria's legs. "You have to kill someone."

"Huh?" JJ blinked at him.

Bony grinned. "That's all there is to it. We have to know you really want to be with us. Friends for life, see."

"Friends for life!" Sammy squeaked. He touched knuckles with Eduardo.

JJ shook his head. "You're joking, right?"

Eduardo's eyes narrowed. His smile faded. "It's not a joke, man. It's serious. That's the initiation."

JJ let out a long whoosh of air. "Too heavy for me, man." He started to his feet.

Maria tugged him back down. "We all did it," she said.

"You telling me you all killed someone to join your club?"

"It's easy, man," Sammy said. "We'll give you the gun and everything."

"I don't think so," JJ said. He realized his chest suddenly felt fluttery. His stomach churned.

Maria ran a fingernail down his cheek. It made his whole body tingle. "You can do it, baby," she whispered. She let her hair brush his cheek again.

"We'll be there for you, man," Sammy said. "Friends for life. Really."

"Here's what you do," Bony said, pulling up more grass, letting it fall in his own lap. "Pick someone, right? Pick some jerk you really don't like. Wait till he's alone. Make sure no one can see. And—*POP*. That's all there is to it. It's cake."

Maria squeezed his hand. Her breath tickled his face.

"This is the gun," Eduardo said. He held up a tiny pistol, not much bigger than a cell phone. "Cute, right? But it does the damage."

"We've all used it," Sammy said. "*POP*. That's it. Then you bring it back to us."

"I used to shoot back in Texas," JJ said. Why did his voice suddenly sound so tight, so shrill? "But I used real guns. Not toys like that."

"It'll do the damage," Eduardo repeated. "It's loaded for you, man. It's ready."

JJ took the pistol from him and rolled it in his hand. It felt cool and light. Like a toy. He pictured Florian.

POP.

Florian.

POP.

Florian.

POP.

Florian.

POP.

"Okay," he told them. "I'll do it."

Sometimes days fly past like the wind. Here it was, three nights later, and JJ, sweating despite the evening cool, found the four Killers at the familiar place in the park, deep shadows playing over their expectant faces.

"I did it." The words burst from his mouth in a breathy explosion. He raised the pistol in front of him. It glinted in a narrow beam of moonlight. "Friends for life, right?"

He waited for them to react. To congratulate him. Some high fives. Some knuckle slaps. So, why the silent treatment?

"You don't believe me?" JJ shoved the pistol back into his jeans. He leaned against a tree trunk and stared down at them. "I did it. Just like you said. I killed Florian. Shot him in the head."

More silence. Sammy and Eduardo exchanged glances. Maria bit her bottom lip.

"I waited for the restaurant to close," JJ said. "There was no one around. The parking lot was totally dark.

I walked up behind him and shot him in the head. He dropped onto the trunk of his car. Didn't know what hit him."

Maria let out a gasp. She looked away.

"You shot him?" Bony said finally. He kept blinking. "You really shot him?"

JJ nodded.

"But we loaded the gun with blanks," Sammy squeaked.

"Yeah. Tell me about it," JJ said. "I took the pistol to a firing range to try it out. All six chambers were loaded with blanks. So I bought a box of bullets for it. Guess you guys messed up."

"No way," Bony said, shaking his head. "It was *supposed* to be blanks, JJ. You weren't supposed to kill anyone. It was just a joke, see. The whole thing was a joke."

JJ's eyes grew wide. He opened his mouth, but no words came out.

"It was a joke, dude," Eduardo said. "We're not killers. We didn't kill anyone. You're the new kid. You looked so desperate. We thought we'd have some fun with you, that's all."

"Fun?" JJ said in a whisper. *"Fun?"*

"We were messing with you, man," Bony said. "We were punking you."

"Why did you put real bullets in the gun?" Maria cried. "You weren't supposed to!" She had tears in her eyes, and her chin quivered. "You weren't supposed to kill anyone."

JJ slammed his open hand against the tree trunk. "Oh, please . . . Oh, please, oh, please. I killed Florian. You told me I had to. Now you tell me it's a joke? But it's NOT a joke! I *killed* him!"

"JJ, sit down," Maria said, tears running down her cheeks. She patted the grass beside her. "We have to talk about this. All of us."

JJ didn't move from the tree trunk. "I'm a *murderer*," he uttered in a low, trembling voice. "A murderer, all because of a *joke*."

"But no one saw you, right?" Sammy asked. "There's no way anyone knows it was you, JJ."

JJ shut his eyes tight. His jaw clenched and unclenched. The others watched him in silence. "No. No one saw me," he said finally. "No one knows . . ."

His eyes opened wide. "Except you guys. You're the only ones who know I killed him. You're, like, witnesses or something."

He stepped away from the tree. His whole body stiffened. He jammed his hand into his jeans pocket and brought out the pistol.

"Hey, don't get crazy," Bony said. He jumped up from the grass. He took a step toward JJ. "We're not going to snitch on you, man."

"No, you're *not* going to snitch on me," JJ said softly. He pointed the pistol at Bony. "I won't let you snitch on me."

Maria scrambled to her feet and took a few steps back, eyes wary. "JJ, what are you doing? JJ—please. Put it down."

"I can't trust you," JJ said. "I can't trust any of you. Everything you told me was a lie."

"Listen to us. It was supposed to be a joke—" Bony said.

"I'm a murderer because of you," JJ repeated, sweat pouring down his forehead. He waved the pistol from Bony to Maria, then down to the other two boys, still hunched tensely in the grass. "A murderer—and you're the only ones who know."

"We won't tell. Promise!" Sammy whined.

"JJ—don't," Maria pleaded. "Put down the gun. This is crazy."

JJ shook his head. "You understand me, right? You all have to take a bullet. I can't trust you. No way. I can't take a chance."

He aimed the pistol at Bony. His arm tensed.

Maria let out a scream.

Bony jumped at JJ. He made a wild grab for the gun.

JJ swiped it out of Bony's reach—and fired.

POP.

Bony uttered a groan. His face showed more surprise than pain. He grabbed his stomach, dropped face-first to the grass, landed with a soft thud, bounced once, then didn't move.

Maria screamed again. The scream ended in a choking gasp.

Sammy and Eduardo were on their feet. They had their arms outstretched, partially in surrender. Their faces were twisted in fright.

"Who's next?" JJ barked, hoarse, excited. He swung the pistol from one to the other. "Who's next?"

"Please—" Sammy wailed. "Please—"

"Don't kill us," Eduardo said. "You can trust us. Really. We won't tell anyone."

Maria stared at him silently, her hair falling over her face. She was breathing hard, her chest heaving up and down. "JJ—no." Her voice a faint whisper.

"Please don't kill us," Sammy said again. "We'll be your friends. Really."

JJ laughed. He lowered the pistol to his side. "Guess your initiation is over. You made it."

Sammy and Eduardo froze. Their eyes bulged, studying JJ. Maria hugged herself tightly, her whole body shuddering.

"Initiation?" Sammy finally choked out.

JJ nodded. "Yeah. If you want to hang with me, you have to pass *my* initiation. Bony and I cooked it up." He spun the pistol on his thumb. "All blanks. Nothing but blanks." He chuckled again. "That got a little tense, huh?"

The other three still weren't taking it in. You could almost see the thoughts whirring in their heads.

"You punked *us*?" Eduardo said finally.

JJ nodded. "Bony and I. It was kinda his idea."

"You didn't kill Florian?" Maria asked, brushing her damp hair off her forehead. "That was a lie?"

"A lie," JJ said. "All a joke. I should be an actor or something, right? I was pretty good."

"You're both creeps!" Maria shouted. "You scared us to death!"

"Is the initiation over?" Eduardo asked. His gaze was on the pistol in JJ's hand.

"Yeah. It's over," JJ said. "Friends for life, right?" He turned to Bony, still on his stomach on the grass. "Get up, man. We're done. It's a done deal. We punked these dudes. They're still shaking."

Bony didn't move. His hands were tucked beneath him, still gripping his stomach. His face was down in the dirt.

JJ gave him a gentle kick in the side. "Come on, Bony. Stop clowning. Get up, man. Let's get out of here."

Bony didn't move.

JJ gave him another soft kick with the toe of his boot.

Bony's body bounced once, then settled back in place.

"Bony, no! No! Bony?" Maria began to scream.

JJ dropped to his knees. He grabbed Bony's jacket and flipped him onto his back. Bony's hands fell limply away from his body. A lopsided puddle of dark blood stained the front of his T-shirt.

"Bony—no! No! Bony—no!"

Bony's eyes gazed blankly at the sky, glassy and un-blinking.

"What happened?" JJ wailed in a high, shrill voice. "They were blanks. They were all blanks. What happened?"

"Y-you *killed* him!" Sammy whispered. "You shot Bony in the stomach!"

A hoarse cry escaped JJ's throat. "No. I couldn't. They were blanks. I know they were. All blanks. Bony and I cooked it up. It was a joke!"

Shaking his head, JJ began murmuring to himself in a panic. "Oh, wow. Oh, wow. Bony dead? I killed Bony? It couldn't happen. It couldn't. Oh, wow. Oh, wow."

Bony laughed. He blinked a few times and sat up with a grin on his face. He slapped JJ's arm. "Gotcha, dude. That was *your* initiation!"

JJ made a choking sound. The others burst out laughing.

Sammy helped Bony to his feet. "Good one, dude."

JJ stood up on shaky legs and narrowed his eyes at them. "You were all in on it? From beginning to end? You all knew about this . . . this joke?"

Maria wiped tears from her eyes. This time, they were tears of laughter. The others slapped knuckles, tossed their heads back, and howled at the moon.

"They were all in on it, dude," Bony told him. "Don't you get it? It wasn't their initiation. It was *your* initiation!"

"You were punked, JJ!" Eduardo cried.

"You should have seen the look on your face!"

They howled some more. Bony hugged Maria around the waist. Sammy and Eduardo did a wild victory dance around the tree.

They stopped when they saw someone running toward them. Her hair flew wildly behind her head, and the wind lifted her coat as she stumbled over the wet grass.

JJ recognized her immediately. "Julie!" He turned to the others. "The waitress from the restaurant."

He took a few steps toward her. She stopped, hands balled into tense fists. She took a few deep breaths.

"Julie—how did you find me? What's up?"

"You won't believe this, JJ," Julie said, her jaw clenched, eyes wide. "Florian is dead."

JJ heard Maria gasp.

"Someone shot him in the head," Julie said. "They found him in the parking lot. He's dead. Someone *killed* him!" Her body shuddered. She wrapped her arms around herself.

Bony stepped up to JJ and grabbed him by the shirt collar. "This is another joke, right?" His eyes burned into JJ's. "The waitress is in on it, right? This is another initiation joke?"

JJ stared back at Bony and smiled.

She's Different Tonight

· HEATHER GRAHAM ·

It was Halloween.

And what a Halloween.

You have to understand, I really, *really*, love Halloween.

Such a perfect night was truly rare. The weather was balmy, almost warm, but kissed with a cool breeze. The sky had been crystal clear all day, blue, beautifully blue.

And a full moon was about to rise high. It had begun its ascent already. Soon, it would be luminous across a black velvet heaven. I mean, conditions could not have been more perfect.

I was dressed like a football player, and it was the perfect costume for me, honestly. Not to sound too cocky, but I can pull off a jock pretty well. I have the old all-American, farm-raised, blue-eyed, wheaten-haired boy-next-door appeal; I'm pretty tall—six three—and I have broad shoulders before adding the pads in. I looked like the real deal. All-American, the boy-next-door. Funny. I was anything but.

She happened to be at the service bar just as I was, and since I'd seen her around before, I knew her to be usually shy and mild-mannered. She hung with a crowd that was kind of on the edge—close to, but not quite in with—the elite. The kind always hoping to get in. To get closer to those of us who glowed with the esteem and admiration we received from others. Knowing *me* would be a notch in her belt. She might be willing to do just about anything for the privilege of saying that we were . . . *friends.* That she had been with me, on Halloween night.

Perfect.

She was just perfect.

I'd been watching her, you see. I'd been contemplating this night. Then, tonight, I'd been watching again. Making sure she'd come alone, and was trying to fit in. Tonight, here, I'd been watching again with patience, knowing that I was stalking her, but keeping in mind as well that I needed to find the perfect *date*, to make sure that it was her.

The perfect date.

Someone who drew little notice.

Someone not easily missed.

And that *was* her. Usually.

This Halloween, though, it seemed she was playing against type.

And it worked for her. No more dowdy little schoolgirl, bordering on the nerdy. I was pleasantly surprised by her wickedly erotic appeal. The good girl, all dressed up as if she were bad.

Like I said, I'd seen her around before, I *stalked* her. She always had an armload of books. She usually wore glasses, and they were often slipping down her nose. She was the studious type. *A mouse.* She kind of hunched forward when she walked, hugging those books of hers. She was a good girl who had left home and gone on to college to do the folks proud. I always thought she must have come off a farm. You'd think *nerd*, and you'd be right. But I have to admit, though I hadn't given it much thought before, there had always been something appealing about her. Something delicious in the scent of her. And tonight . . . well, she had almost pitch-black hair to begin with. Long and straight. And she had the kind of hazel eyes that—

with the contact lenses she was wearing—really took on an honest-to-God, snakelike, vampire appearance. Very cool. She was wearing a dress that might have done Morticia or Vampira proud; it hugged her body, her every curve. It was as if she were breaking out of some kind of shell, and a better man than I might have been hard-pressed to resist. Who had ever imagined the figure beneath those books, beneath the gawky stance? And yet she was still . . . well, the same girl. The same girl who needed me.

And, as I already admitted, I had been watching. Eyeing her. Not quite imagining this, but planning out my moves, you might say.

"Hey," I said.

"Hey," she replied, just a little startled that I had talked to her.

"Great costume," I said.

"You too."

"It's just a football thing," I said.

Her lips curled in a smile. "One would think you might have dressed up like a wolf," she said.

Ouch. So she did have a sense of humor.

"Who'd have thought *you*'d be the sexy undead?" I whispered, my tone very flattering.

"Oh, well. Life *can* be pretense and dress-up," she said.

She sounded breathless. In fact, it was great. She almost looked as if she were going to swoon.

"Need some air?" I asked her.

She looked at me, surprised once again. I think she might have blushed—hard to tell in that makeup she was wearing. Fake lashes? Or were those her own, touched with mascara?

This was like a fascinating miracle. She was actually stunning tonight. Seductive and clever. Witty. And the way she looked in the tight getup, I hadn't been lying. She was sexy. Sensuous. Hot.

She looked downward for a moment and I knew she was thinking quickly. Maybe her heart was even fluttering. After all, I was one of the most popular kids in school. Okay, I admit—I come from a lot of money. I drive a cool car. But the rest, I'd done on my own. I have a certain amount of charm and pure *animal* appeal. She was thinking, *Wow, me! Vince Romero has singled me out of the crowd!*

Okay, I think I've admitted, I might be a little on the cocky side, too.

She looked up at me. "Air," she said simply.

"Yeah, it's getting stuffy in here," I said with a shrug. "Shall we slip away?" I was my most seductive self. I'd never quite imagined it like this. That I'd be more than playing, teasing. But I wasn't jarred or thrown off. I was simply enjoying.

She stared at me for a moment. I almost smiled. She looked the part, but she wasn't quite there. She was like a deer caught in headlights. She seemed to tremble. Then she nodded. Just as if she'd been hypnotized.

"Um, you did come alone?" I asked.

"Yeah." Such a sweet, throaty note in her voice. "And . . . you? You came alone?" she asked.

Okay, so I usually had a blonde with size quadruple-D bazoongas on my arm.

I smiled. "I've been waiting for you all night. I've watched you, you know."

"Oh," she breathed, staring at me. "Really?"

"Really," I assured her.

She flushed with pleasure and looked away for a moment. "You know," she admitted, "I've been watching you, too."

"Really?" I countered.

"Really," she said. "I guess . . . well, I guess you didn't notice. People are watching you all the time."

I shrugged, but smiled, and placed my hand at the small of her back.

We slipped out the back door. I was careful. No one saw us.

"Hey, my car is right over there. And I have a six-pack in a cooler in the back," I told her. I had noticed that she was carrying a draft beer.

She looked up at me. Those eyes of hers were wicked tonight. "I'm sure you do," she said.

"Be prepared," I said. "That's my motto."

She laughed again. The sound was throaty. Sexy. Wow. It was going to be a good night. Oh, yes. Halloween. A full moon. This little wishy-washy girl suddenly looking like a *Cosmo* girl. It was all right. And she just had no idea.

I felt my blood heating up. This was going to be an easy conquest. Easier than I had imagined.

I slipped an arm around her shoulders as we walked to the car. There was a full moon out. Cool. Too cool. You didn't get a full moon on Halloween all that often.

We reached the car.

"Want to drive?" I asked her.

"Sure." She sounded a little breathless.

It was such a great pickup. Everyone wanted to drive my car. It was a jazzed-up sports car, an Audi with a few custom alterations. Friends drooled to have my car. And she was getting to drive it.

I opened the driver-side door for her, and she slid in. I bounded around to the passenger's seat and hopped in beside her. She was running her fingers over the leather seat. "Nice," she told me.

"Thanks. Ivanna Romanoff," I said, rolling her name pleasantly on my tongue. "Pretty name."

"I'm glad you like it," she told me. I was a little surprised. After the first sign of shock she'd shown, she'd begun gaining some confidence. Maybe she knew that she was nerdy, but—now that she was in the proper attire—dynamite-looking and totally alluring without her hunch-over-her-books and down-on-the-nose glasses.

"Russian?" I asked her.

She waved a hand in the air. "Oh, well, I guess my ancestors were from Eastern Europe, somewhere. Vince Romero. Spanish? Italian?"

I smiled. "Eastern European, too," I said. "But, hey, maybe that means we're meant for each other, huh? Romero—Romanoff. Not that far off."

"Not that far off at all," she said, nodding.

"There you have it—two unique, mysterious pasts!" I said.

"Oh, quite." She laughed. "And we both have New England accents," she said.

"Hey, ain't that America? Land of opportunity," I said.

The moon was rising. It was getting later.

Surely, she must know that she was being seduced—no matter how naïve she might have appeared at times.

I was cool, after all.

I found myself realizing that she was close, that she was wearing a truly exotic perfume. Her body was warm, enticing. She had moved even a little closer to me—no, I had moved a little closer to her. That perfume. Wow. It was seductive.

I almost felt guilty.

Almost. In fact, I was so close to guilt, I could taste it.

I tamped down the feeling. It was Halloween. It was perfect. All was going according to plan.

"I always thought of you as shy," I murmured.

"I guess I am shy, usually. It's just that . . . well, I've heard about you. I've watched you, as I told you, and the girls talk, of course," she told me.

Was it kind of a come-on? Was I supposed to prove that I was as studly as she had heard?

I leaned back, smiling. I let my fingers play in that long, silky black hair of hers. How odd—I mean, it was her hair. The same hair she had every day. Tonight . . . it was electric. So sleek and shiny it almost gleamed blue.

"Where am I going?" she asked.

"Huh?"

"I love driving your car, but where should I drive to?"

"Somewhere quiet. Where we can be alone," I said.

Too much? Would she bolt?

"Well, where would you be going if you were driving?" she asked.

"Quiet where we won't be disturbed . . ." I murmured, as if I were deep in thought. I looked at her. "I know. The cemetery."

"Oh."

"Does it disturb you? I mean, if so—"

"Oh, no," she said. "I like cemeteries. They're full of history."

"They're full of the dead," I couldn't help but say.

Her sweet, teasing smile slipped back to her lips. "History," she said stubbornly. "Cemeteries are filled with stories, and with lives gone by, and history."

"Sure."

She drove straight to the cemetery far out on Main Street. She was right about the history. The cemetery went way back; heroes from the Revolutionary War were buried in it. Hell, there was a grave that belonged to a fellow who had come over on the *Mayflower*. There was a small church way down on the western side, so I guess that meant it was officially called a graveyard rather than a cemetery; but the church was one of the oldest buildings in our area, and it was small, locked tight at night. In fact, the structure, standing kind of forlorn in the cool moonlight, made it all the better.

The point here is that the place was old, spooky, and neat. There was a wall around it, an old stone wall. But the wall was about two feet high. I had a blanket and the cooler in back. It was mild for October.

Perfect. Once again, I counted my blessings. All things were—perfect.

"We're going *into* the cemetery?" she asked.

"Dead people are the safest people in the world, you know. They won't hurt you," I told her. "You just said that you liked cemeteries—they're filled with history and great stories about lives gone past."

"That's in the daytime," she said, shaking her head. But she was just watching me—she wasn't really protesting.

"Have you ever been in a cemetery at night?" I asked.

"Maybe," she said coyly.

Maybe. Oh, she was lying.

She shivered slightly.

"We can go somewhere else. I mean, believe it or not, I just kind of love the peace around here, and the . . . the quiet," I said. I was surprised. I sounded a little lame.

She looked at me and smiled slowly. "Well, I will be with you."

"You are certainly safe with the folks in a cemetery," I said. "Graveyard. Whatever."

Of course, in my mind, I was being totally honest. None of the folks in their graves would do her any harm.

So we gathered up the cooler and a blanket, exited the car, and hopped over the wall. I helped her, of course, setting my hands around her to lift her over the wall, realizing as I did so just how perfect a little figure she had. Tiny waist, and flaring curves above and below. I'd have never imagined that she was so finely honed, that she obviously worked out, that she was such a piece of physical perfection.

That word again. *Perfect.*

Not a bad night's work.

We found a place beneath a huge old oak and spread out the blanket. She sat with me and I noticed her drink was gone; I popped the tab on a dark Irish beer and offered it to her. She drank, watching me, those snakelike vampire eyes getting a golden glow in them that was truly exciting. I sipped my beer, I looked to the sky, and then I kissed her. It was great. She was hesitant, a little shy still, despite her demeanor. I pressed her downward, savoring the feel of her heat and the shivering within her.

Then it started. The transformation.

I felt it tear and burn through me, and with Ivanna in my arms, the rip in my muscles, the fire in my blood, and the savage hunger in my heart were just about orgasmic. Soon, she would scream. She would see the shoulder pads fall away, the football breeches stretch and tear, and she would know the true concept of a guy who was an *animal*. I felt the first magnificent howl that the moon was eliciting form in my throat.

Yes, I was transforming. . . .

The all-American boy into . . .

The all-American werewolf.

I did have to be careful. I was living in the modern world, of course, here in America. I actually wanted to get my college degree and enter the truly savage arena of corporate law. So I did date, and I was a stud, and I didn't rip and tear apart all those women who befriended me. But, hell, it was Halloween, and a Halloween with a full moon. I'd been extremely watchful that night; I'd caught her at the service bar, and I knew that we'd exited without anyone seeing us.

I looked down. I looked down longing for that look in her eyes; that look that meant terror and knowledge. But, usually, it had something a little more. Something that told me a woman knew of *her own death*, and yet her sexuality was at such a heightened peak that she would die in the throes of an ecstatic excitement. And the look in her eyes would be ecstasy in and of itself for me. . . .

This isn't boasting. This isn't arrogance, or conceit. It is what I am, and what the beast within is capable of creating.

And the sensation that would follow for me . . .

Ah, it would be wondrous.

Not to mention the soul-shattering wonder of the kill.

But her eyes weren't full of terror—or excitement. She was staring at me with amusement. Total amusement.

And she started to laugh.

I had never known that laughter would ruin everything. That it would *stop* the transformation.

"Don't you know what I am? Don't you *see?*" I demanded.

To my astonishment, she pushed at my chest—with a stunning power. I halfway fell back. I stared at her, thinking that my fury would start the transformation all over again.

But she leaped atop me, and her laughter tore from her like a banshee's cackle in the night, and to my amaze-

ment, I discovered that I was pinned beneath her. *Pinned!*
Me!

"Don't you know what *I* am? Can't *you* see?" she demanded with a throaty chuckle. "You are in costume
tonight, and I, finally, am not! Oh, the poor little book-
worm! The shy girl—who should fall all over herself for
a chance to be with the hot guy. Oh, what a silly, silly
egoist of a dumb animal you are!"

I opened my mouth to speak, but no words came.

Above me, I saw the moon, the beautiful full moon.

That was when she leaned forward and bit me.

Sank her fangs into my flesh and began to slurp.

And beneath that beautiful full moon, I heard the hor-
rid sucking sounds she made, and I felt my blood, my life,
my magnificent life, being drained away.

It was Halloween.

And what a Halloween. . . .

Not quite so . . .

Perfect.

SUCKERS

· SUZANNE WEYN ·

· NEW YORK, 2060 ·

It wasn't that I didn't want to ever visit the tiny planet of Lectus; I just didn't want to live there. I mean, who wants to move at the end of his junior year of high school? You just don't ask a guy to do something like that. I was set to go to the junior prom with Stephy Hoppington. She was counting on me. And on July Fourth I was planning my first skydive with my pals. I'd already put a deposit down on the plane ride.

But my family isn't like other families because Dad and Mom are actors, not just regular thespians, either. Biggs and Julie Boreidae are both movie stars, the kind that appear on the cover of cheap newspapers at the grocery store checkout line with headlines that announce every month that their marriage is ending. *Splitsville* is the way one magazine put it last March.

These reports were obviously bogus. Mom and Dad were more together as a couple than the parents of anyone else I knew. (Which maybe isn't saying much, but still . . .)

The weird press and the fact that family was important to Mom and Dad was partly the reason Dad decided to relocate us to Lectus, supposedly the newest, hottest place for the elite to set up residence. He wanted the family to be someplace more private; "away from the ever-prying eyes of the paparazzi," was how he put it.

My school, Flemont Prep, has some real rich kids in it, but, just the same, all my friends were super impressed that we were going to Lectus. Real estate on Lectus costs so much that only billionaires could afford it. But with Mom and Dad's combined star power they were able to buy a private ranch on the newly terra-formed planet at the outer edge of the solar system—plus first-class tickets on the new, high-speed, luxury space transport, *Gattus*.

Not one of us four kids wanted to go. My older sister, Felicia, cried day and night until her face was permanently puffed. My younger twin brothers, Chester and Chomper, weren't any happier. (We gave Chomper that nickname because as a baby he liked to bite everything in sight.) I tried to reason with Dad about the inconvenience of living so far away from the movie industry, but Chester and Chomper just plain-out begged, pleading not to be taken from their friends.

I don't think Mom was even really that thrilled about the move, but she was philosophical about it. "Lectus is supposed to be gorgeous," she said, trying to console us, "and it's a wonderful hopping-off point to some of the really desirable other planets that are so popular these days as movie locations. Dad and I can be home much more often this way."

We were standing on the docking platform when *Gattus* came into view. I had to admit, the huge space transport was something to see. It was so gigantic I felt like a microbe standing next to it. And it had these two giant, green headlights in front. As it descended into its transport dock its engine purred steadily.

"All aboard, kids," Dad instructed as we crossed the walkway. When we reached *Gattus*, we entered a dark walkway. It was soft and the floor was cushiony under my feet.

"What is this?" I asked Dad.

"It's a bio-transport," Dad explained. "All our biological needs are built right into the structure of the ship."

"Do you mean I could bite this floor and there would be food in it?" I asked in disbelief.

"Yep."

"Weird," I mumbled.

In no time at all, we arrived at our new home on the planet Lectus. As the transport docked, an uneasy feeling overcame me. Maybe it's just fear of the unknown, I told myself. How I wish now that that had been true.

As soon as we disembarked, a space bus whizzed us out to our ranch. It was a vast expanse, but there wasn't much livestock other than a few goats. Huge white tumbleweeds blew across the flat acreage. "It doesn't look like much now, but once we've had a chance to fix it up, you're going to love it," Dad said, opening the front doors to our new home.

As I stepped inside the big, empty ranch house, I wasn't so sure. That eerie feeling was still with me and rattling around this huge, vacant place wasn't helping.

"Let's go home," Chester requested. "I don't like it here."

"Me neither," Felicia seconded him.

"Give it a chance," Mom said. "Once we move our belongings in it'll feel more like home."

That night, I tried to call Stephy, but as I'd suspected, the satellite signal didn't reach back home. Felicia must have discovered this at the same time I did because I heard her shouting from her new bedroom: "This is Hell! We are living in Hell now!"

The next day couldn't have been more boring. There was no one around. I actually missed going to school! Desperate for something to do, I wandered to the farthest edge of our property and was really happy to discover another luxurious ranch house very like ours. At least we weren't completely alone out here.

I approached nervously, feeling awkward about just introducing myself to strangers. I came up on a grassy hill behind my new house and from there I could see into the yard. My nearest neighbors had a pool, and someone was floating in it.

Feeling encouraged because I wouldn't actually have to knock on the door in order to meet my new neighbors, I quickened my pace. As I got closer, I saw that the person floating there in the pool was possibly the most beautiful girl I had ever seen.

She looked to be about my age, maybe a little younger, but not much. This girl was too awesome to be real. For a moment I was sure I was dreaming. The sun glistened off her dark hair. And, her skimpy bikini revealed a figure that made all thoughts of Stephy Hoppington fly out of my head.

"Hi, I'm Phil," I said as I climbed over the split-rail fence separating our properties. "I just moved into the ranch next to yours."

She swam to the pool's edge and propped herself up on her elbows; her brown eyes studied me in a languid, sleepy kind of way. "I'm Etchenia."

"Pretty name."

"Thanks."

She was so beautiful.

"Is school done for the season?" I asked. "I'd sort of like to meet some other kids."

Etchenia shook her head. "Everyone has private tutors on Lectus."

"Why?"

"Kidnapping," she answered in a low, secretive tone.

"What?" I asked.

Etchenia nodded. "Kids around here sometimes just disappear. Older people, too." She snapped her fingers. "Whole groups of people—entire neighborhoods. Poof! Gone. Just like that."

"Has anyone ever demanded a ransom?" I asked. I figured that the reason for the kidnappings was because Lectus was such a wealthy planet.

Etchenia shook her head. "Never. And no one has ever come back."

"Wow," I murmured. Suddenly it occurred to me that maybe she was a little crazy. Could what she was telling me be true? It seemed impossible.

But she was so hot and gorgeous that I desperately hoped she wasn't also a loon. "With all these disappearances, aren't you scared to be out in the pool all alone?"

"I'm not alone." She gestured back to the house and, for the first time, I noticed armed guards dressed entirely in black stationed on two of the balconies. "Telescopic, long-range rifles," she reported.

Instinctively, I backed away from her.

"Don't worry," she assured me with a twinkling laugh. "I have a hand signal for danger, and I didn't give it."

"I didn't know Lectus was such a dangerous place."

"I know. The real estate people don't tell you until you're already here. Lectus is a very weird place. It's not so bad these days, not like before."

"What happened before?"

"Nothing. Forget it. It was a long time ago. I was just a little kid. My father managed to take us off the planet for the worst of it. He thinks it's safe again now, but . . ." She glanced back at the bodyguards stationed on the balconies. "He's not taking any chances."

"Did anyone ever figure out who was causing the disappearances?"

She shook her head. "Nope."

"Strange. Want to come over to my house sometime?" I asked.

"When?"

"Tonight?"

"Sure. Eight o'clock okay?"

"Sure. It's right over there," I said, pointing.

"See you at eight."

Etchenia arrived promptly, with two armed guards at her side. Dressed in a short, flowing white sundress, she looked unbelievable.

Chomper answered the door. "Phil, your girlfriend is here!" he bellowed.

"Shut up!" I said, bopping him on the head as I came to the door. "Hi!"

Etchenia left the guards outside and stepped in. My parents came down the stairs to see who had come in. "Oh, my gosh! Biggs and Julie Boreidae!" Etchenia gasped. She turned to me. "Why didn't you tell me that's your last name?"

"Because people act the way you just did," I explained.

"Oh, sorry."

"Not at all," Mom told her. "We love to meet our fans, don't we, Biggs?" She was using her silky movie-star voice.

"Can't have enough fans," Dad agreed spryly. His shoulders were back and his chin up. It was his public stance, the one he took out when he played the assortment of heroic types he'd built his career on. He was always cast as a brave policeman, a fearless astronaut, a noble superhero, a brilliant detective; whatever the role, Dad's character always saved the day.

A worried expression suddenly swept over Etchenia's face. "You didn't tell your other movie-star friends about Lectus, did you?"

"No, but a story about it ran in *The Daily Snitch*," Mom told her. "Why do you look so worried?"

"Lectus just isn't as nice when it gets crowded," Etchenia said. "That's when the scary things start happening."

"They have kidnappings here," I said. "Disappearances, whatever you want to call it. Did you know about that?"

"No," Dad admitted, looking concerned.

"There are other things, too," Etchenia said, seeming very distressed.

"Like what?" Mom asked.

Etchenia wrung her delicate hands. "I really don't want to talk about it. I should be going."

"But you just got here," I protested. "Tell us what the other scary things are."

"I'm sorry." She headed for the door, pulling it open. Her bodyguards closed in beside her and stayed that way as she hurried down the front walk.

"Maybe we should have bodyguards, too," I suggested as I watched her go.

"We came here to get away from the need for bodyguards," Dad reminded me. "Are you sure she isn't a little . . ." He tapped his forehead. "You know . . . unreliable."

"Phil's girlfriend is wacky!" Chompers shouted gleefully from his spying place behind the couch.

"Shut up," I told him. I turned back to Dad. "I don't know. The thought occurred to me," I admitted. "The whole bit about overpopulation bringing on the bad stuff *is* kind of strange."

"It is. And I wouldn't worry about overpopulation, anyway," Dad said. "Right now I haven't seen anyone for miles."

"Speaking of overpopulation, I guess this is a good time to tell you," Mom said, smiling. "Lectus is about to get a bit more populated. I went to the doctor this morning. I'm pregnant—with triplets!"

Every day the holographic TV showed footage of *Gattus* arriving at the Lectus transport dock—its four thick landing columns set firmly on the planet before the body of the transport settled down over them, its purring engine so steady and relentless—and then more and more new arrivals streaming off.

Remembering what Etchenia had said, I was alarmed at how quickly the population was climbing. Added to that, half the women in Lectus seemed to be pregnant. Mom joined a support group called Mothers of Multiples. "The meetings are more packed every time," she reported one evening after returning from a meeting.

Dad was composing a spoken letter into his recorder, and he switched it off. "That's because the news has spread that *you're* there, Julie. Don't forget you're a movie star. They've all come out to see you."

"I don't know," Mom disagreed. "There are some very full-looking women there and a lot of them."

Felicia glanced up from the couch, where she was perusing a beauty magazine of some sort. "They're probably stuffing themselves with padding just to see you," she commented.

"Hmm. I'm not sure," Mom murmured.

"Well, I'm sending a letter of protest to the agents who sold us this ranch," Dad said. "They have oversold the property here. We're being inundated with the very crowds we came to escape. I can only think they've dropped their prices sharply. How else can so many newcomers be able to afford it here?"

It was amazing how fast things were changing. McMansions began popping up everywhere you looked. One day there would be an empty field and by the next morning there would be a huge house on it. The roads were clogged with giant trucks dragging prefabricated homes behind them. They clicked together like enormous LEGOs.

I tried to get in touch with Etchenia by hanging around by her pool since I didn't have her phone number. I couldn't go to her front door because the guards wouldn't let me pass by.

Finally, I did come upon her swimming in her pool. With my eyes on the guards watching from the balconies, I hopped the fence, hoping Etchenia wouldn't give them her secret danger hand signal.

Etchenia swam to the edge of the pool, though she wouldn't look at me. "Why did you run off that day?" I asked directly.

"When I heard your mother was pregnant, I knew it was starting again," she replied.

"What?"

"The births, the crowding, I just can't stand to live through it again. Even though I was a child, I still remember." Her voice was climbing to a hysterical pitch.

"You really think the disappearances will start again?" I asked.

"I don't want to talk about any of it. You'll find out for yourself. My parents are planning to leave Lectus as soon as they can sell the ranch. Tell your family to leave, too."

I nodded. "Okay. Does your father really think it's not safe now?" I was on the trail of something. Maybe Etchenia had this irrational fear and her father *knew* it was all in her head. What if the bodyguards were just there to calm her fears?

"When Daddy married my stepmom, she wanted to come here and Daddy isn't able to say no to her about anything. But now we've convinced her to leave, too."

"Maybe whatever it was won't happen again," I suggested. "Your father thought it was safe to return. You were little. You could have misunderstood what was going on."

"Maybe," she conceded, though she looked unconvinced. "I'm not going to talk about it anymore. Please go away." She dove under the surface.

I waited for her to come up again. I had so many questions. But she stayed under, swimming in circles, for a very long time.

Movement up on the balcony made me nervous, so I went back to my side of the fence and headed home.

That evening was warm. I was in the yard watching Chester and Chomper on the swings. Mom and Dad were in the house, and Felicia was out with friends. Friends were no longer in short supply. I had made a few myself but nobody that I really clicked with. No one else seemed to be worried about Etchenia's strange disappearance stories, or had even heard of them, for that matter.

Coming across the yard, I saw a figure walking toward me in the dusky light. It was Etchenia. I noticed she seemed to wobble unsteadily. I ran to meet her. As I got closer I could see that she was frighteningly pale with dark circles under her eyes.

"What's wrong? Where are your guards?"

"Passed out. Maybe dead. My parents, too."

"What?" I asked incredulously.

"It's started at the north end, closer to my place, but it's headed your way. I had to come warn you."

"What do you mean?" I asked.

Etchenia staggered into me, clutching my arm to support herself. "It's in the air," she said in a raspy voice. "Can't you smell it?"

Lifting my head, I realized she was right—a perfumed

smell, not completely bad, almost like a lily. And just as I became aware of it, I began to feel its effects, too. My lips and tongue were tingling; my eyes were burning. A swirl of building nausea was churning in my belly.

I looked over to Chester and Chomper. Both of them sat in their swings barfing between their legs.

I grabbed Etchenia's hand. "Let's get in the house. We can call an ambulance to go to your place."

Etchenia could barely stand, so I put my arms around her shoulders and hurried over to Chomper and Chester. "Get in the house, guys. Come on." They followed Etchenia and me, puking and stumbling all the way.

Inside, Mom and Dad were passed out on the living room couch. Settling Etchenia in a chair, I staggered toward the phone, but my head began to spin and then I fell to my knees. It was the last thing I remembered.

In the morning, I awoke where I'd fallen. Dad was just awakening, rubbing his head. He shook Mom, whose eyes slowly fluttered open. Chomper and Chester lay on the floor. I was relieved to hear Chomper mumble when Dad picked him up. Chester was harder to rouse but finally came to after several very scary moments.

I shook Etchenia but she was cold and lifeless. "Mom! Dad! She's dead!" I shouted.

Dad sprang to my side and checked. "Oh, my God,"

he said, and kept repeating it. Lunging to his phone on the table, he tried to call the police but the lines were busy.

That evening, I went with Dad to a town meeting at the Lectus Center. We were among hundreds of people as we filed into the auditorium. In the afternoon we had learned that Etchenia's entire family was dead, including the bodyguards. Everyone at the north end had been wiped out. On our road, the people had only been sickened.

I sat down feeling sad and scared. I hadn't known Etchenia well, but seeing her there, so still and pale . . . it was horrible. Every time I pictured it, I had to stop myself from shaking.

The head real estate agent on Lectus was a bald-headed guy with a British accent they called Sir Melvin. He was scurrying around shaking hands, trying to do some panic control. The last thing he wanted was a mass exodus off Lectus.

A panel was on the stage and one by one each of them gave his or her opinion about what had happened. A science fiction writer was sure it was an alien attack. The mayor of Lectus felt that some left-leaning newcomers had infiltrated the elite group and had launched a poison gas attack because of a grievance they felt against the massively wealthy of Lectus. An ecologist insisted that Lectus was emitting a natural defense to rid itself of the sudden onslaught of new inhabitants.

When they took comments from the audience, I raised my hand. "I was told that this has happened before."

Members of the panel looked to one another, mystified by my comment. The mayor stood and scratched his head. "I don't know who told you that, son, but I've never heard of it."

Sir Melvin stepped forward. "This settlement has only been terra-formed for the last five years. It's only in the last year that the planet has developed its own ozone layer and the tents have been removed, enabling *Gattus* to land safely."

"Wasn't there a settlement here ten years ago?" I asked.

"Absolutely not. The planet was uninhabitable then."

I knew he was lying. But why? Probably because he thought that real estate sales would plummet if he told the truth about what had happened. At least that was my guess.

"It is a punishment from God!"

All eyes turned to the short, white-haired man in the rumpled black suit. I recognized him from TV and magazines. He was the astronomer Schroeder Peterson. Had it been anyone less highly esteemed, he would have been jeered off the floor. But, since he was the most renowned astronomer in the world, his startling words were met with hushed anticipation.

"A strange light has suddenly and unexpectedly appeared in the sky above Lectus," he explained. "It does not seem to be a star or sun. Possibly it is an alien spacecraft of such immensity we cannot begin to fathom its size. My own belief is that we are being visited by God."

"Why would you think it is God?" Sir Melvin asked respectfully.

"It is just my feeling," Schroeder Peterson replied.

That night we returned home and found Mom and Felicia in Chomper and Chester's room. My brothers were still feeling too sick to get out of bed.

Felicia had stayed at her friend's house that night. When the strange gas came, they had all gone down into their basement, where there were no windows, and hadn't become as overcome with the fumes as most of the other families around us. It was her good luck to have been visiting there at the time.

Dad and I told Mom and Felicia how, by the end of the meeting, Schroeder Peterson had convinced the group that the key to discovering what had happened lay in contacting the light. "They wanted a volunteer to go out in a space module and see if he or she can contact this strange light," Dad told Mom. "No one volunteered. And then someone recognized me and wanted me to go. I guess because I always play the hero part they figured I really am one."

"I hope you said no," Mom told him.

"Of course I did. I sure wasn't going to go and leave you here alone with the kids."

I was actually a little embarrassed by the way Dad had told them that he absolutely wouldn't go. I could tell the others were disappointed that he wasn't living up to his big-screen image.

Dad continued telling about the light and was in midsentence when a deafening roar suddenly split our ears.

The window smashed open, spraying glass everywhere.

I clutched the bedpost with one hand and Chester with the other. A force was pulling us toward the window.

Felicia shrieked as she rose in the air. In an instant she was sucked backward out the window, bumping her head as she went.

Then Chomper began to float upward, flailing his arms and screaming.

Horrified, Mom and Dad reached out to him. Dad, holding on to the bedpost, caught Chomper's ankle.

Mom grabbed Dad around the waist and took hold of Chomper's other leg.

I held tight to Chester as a powerful sucking force lifted me, too. It was as if I was hovering on a current of hot air.

Then came a whine so high-pitched I felt as though my head would shatter. Chester was sucked out of my arms just before I dropped abruptly to the floor.

The last sound I heard was my head banging as it hit.

When I awoke hours later, it was pitch-dark. "Dad?" I whispered as I slowly sat up. "Mom?"

It was eerily quiet. An awful terror gripped me. Had my entire family really just been sucked out the window?

The pain in my head was horrible, but I forced myself to stand and turn on a light.

What I saw made me shake.

The room was completely empty except for one bed that lay on its side. Hurrying to the window, I looked to see if any of them had been dropped to the ground, but no one was there.

I ran outside and thrashed the bushes, calling Mom and Dad, searching for my sister and brothers.

"Phil?"

It was Dad, bleeding and badly scraped, but alive. He

pulled me into an emotional hug. "Thank God you're okay," he said. "Where is everyone else?"

"I can't find them," I told him, my voice catching.

Dad and I searched for hours. We joined a crowd of people also looking for their families who had been swept up by the hot wind. Occasionally, one of them would get lucky and find an injured loved one who had been swept into a tall tree or been blown to a rooftop. But Dad and I couldn't find a trace of Mom, Felicia, Chomper, or Chester.

"What do we do now?" I asked Dad, exhausted and fighting back tears.

"I'm volunteering to go to the light," he said. "If that light has Mom and my kids, I want them back. If I have to finally be a hero for real, then that's what I'll be."

I realized I was sweating. Dad was drenched with perspiration as well. And I was squinting because the sky had turned a vivid, nearly blinding yellow.

I had a front row seat for the launch of the space module being sent to the strange light. The eager, fascinated crowd gathered at the site wearing black sunglasses to protect them from the strong rays of the light.

Dad was already in the module. As he'd walked out

to the pad in his heat-proof spacesuit, he'd looked every inch the hero he always played. I shook his hand and told him how proud I was of him. "Don't worry, Phil. I'll be back," he'd said.

As we waited for the module to take off, a kind of giddiness was overtaking the crowd. It was almost as though they were getting drunk on the light pouring onto us. "I wish I was going, too," an elderly man beside me said.

"Me too. Take me to the light!" a woman shouted, lifting her hands toward it.

"Take me! Take me!" screamed another woman, arms raised, swaying rapturously. Soon everyone was yearning to go toward the light.

A man in a suit tapped me on the shoulder. "Would you like to come into the control room and watch the takeoff on our closed-circuit monitor?" he offered. I thanked him and said I would.

I watched in the darkened room with a handful of technicians as the module took off. "Now we're going to closed-circuit inside the module," a technician with red hair announced.

For a second, I saw Dad sitting at the helm of the cramped cockpit. Then, abruptly, the screen fuzzed before going blank. "We've lost visual," the technician stated the obvious. "The immense heat must be sending solar flares."

"Let's hope the heat panels hold," said the man in the suit.

I sat with my stomach in knots as Dad's voice came into the room. I wished I could've seen him but at least I could hear him.

"I have left Lectus's atmosphere and am heading toward the mysterious light. My solar defense suit is equipped with an internal cooling device. I'm glad of that because already it's scorching up here," he reported.

For several long minutes he was silent.

"As the module gets closer, the light is increasingly blinding. I am flipping the antiglare visor down over my helmet," he said, finally.

"I am attempting to contact the light with a series of laser signals. . . . Nothing."

More silence behind the hum of the speakers.

I wondered why he wasn't speaking.

"The light is just out there," he said, and I noticed that his voice had lost its commanding strength.

"If it is, in fact, God, it is not responding," he spoke again, his voice weaker still.

"I'm not sure what to do next. Even with this suit on, I'm sweating."

I stood, alarmed. "Tell him to come back," I said.

"Can't," the technician said, "we've lost two-way. That light is affecting our communication signals."

"He'll be okay," said the man in the suit.

The next time Dad spoke, he sounded drunk, though I knew he couldn't be. "A strange feeling is taking hold of me—a certainty of what I have to do next," he reported. "It's as if I have no choice anymore. I know this is crazy but I can't stop myself. I am going to the leave the module to go to the light."

"No!" I shouted as a deafening crackle filled the control room.

It is now a year later and I am back on Earth living with my aunt and uncle. They have brought me to a special session of an investigative committee in Washington, D.C.

I sit, anxiously waiting as a senator takes to the podium. "Ladies and gentlemen, this session of our committee is called to order. We have finally recovered the space module flown by John Biggs Boreidae. As you know, for some reason we have yet to understand, the heroic Mr. Boreidae chose to leave his spacecraft in a delusional attempt to go toward the light. However, we have recovered the badly charred module and discovered that its recorder caught these voices. What you are about to hear might be the voices of an alien race far more sophisticated than our own, or as the esteemed Dr. Peterson has suggested, it could, in fact, be the very voice of God."

I sat forward, my fists clenched in anticipation. In the next minute, the module's recorder was played over the public-address system.

Female voice: "Damned fleas! I don't know how we got this infestation. The cat probably brought them in.

"Nothing gets rid of them! I've tried spraying insecticide. I'm sick of vacuuming. The only thing that works at all are these flea traps. They can't help but jump to the lightbulb and then they fall on the sticky paper below.

"It's weird to think that such tough little survivors have such a stupid streak. Who knows why they jump into the light? They just can't help themselves, I guess."

THE PERFECTS

· JENNIFER ALLISON ·

*T*he chances are pretty good that I'm going to be killed before daylight, and I can't help but think this never would have happened if we hadn't moved to Entrails, Michigan. I know there's no point in thinking this way, but really, there's nothing I can *do* but sit here and think. I've already panicked, banged on the bars of my cage, and searched for an escape. Now all I can do is consider how I got into this situation in the first place. Naturally, I find myself wishing I could rewind time—wishing I could go back and redo any of the events and choices that led me to the end of the road.

Did I mention I wouldn't be stuck here now if we

THE PERFECTS · *67*

hadn't moved? That part certainly wasn't *my* choice. My dad lost his job in Detroit and, when neither he nor my mother could find work in their fields, they got the bright idea to move to a small town in the country. My mother managed to find a teaching job but my father's plans were vague: some days he said he planned to start his own business; other days he said he planned to write a bestselling novel or become an organic farmer. At any rate, both of my parents were convinced that out here in Entrails we could live like kings for very little money, and they weren't about to take the advice of a fifteen-year-old girl who didn't want to move.

My parents bought a new house that was about five times the size of our old house in the Detroit suburbs. "And we got it for a song!" my father crowed. It was a foreclosed property; the previous owners had just stopped paying the bills and left town.

Our new house was enormous, but the house next to ours was even bigger—a mansion four stories tall with two towers that popped up from the roof, reminding me of turrets on a medieval castle.

"That house next door is an amazing example of Victorian architecture, Hannah," my mom declared when we first arrived in our new neighborhood.

"Our family and the neighbors next door have the best houses in the whole town," my dad added. "In this town, we're like royalty."

That was the moment I first glimpsed something disturbing—something I did my best to ignore. In an upstairs window of the house next door, a shadowy figure parted the lace curtains and stared down at our car. I had the distinct sense that someone up there was looking at us—sizing us up. But I told myself I was just feeling anxious about being in a new place.

My parents and I went inside to check out the long hallways and empty rooms in our new house. I was trying to decide between two large bedrooms on the second floor when someone rang the doorbell.

I heard my mother open the door.

"Hello. I wanted to welcome you to our neighborhood." It was a woman who spoke with a smooth, formal voice.

Curious, I stepped out of the second-floor bedroom and leaned over the hallway banister to listen more closely.

"My name is Rebecca Perfect," the woman announced. "I live in the house next door."

"Oh, nice to meet you!" In contrast, my mother's voice sounded nasal, high-pitched, and nervous. "Your house is just beautiful!"

From my perch, I saw my mom hurriedly tucking her frizzy hair behind her ears—something she does when she feels embarrassed or intimidated.

"I noticed you have a teenage daughter," said the woman.

"Why, yes. Hannah is fifteen. Hannah, are you up there?" My mother turned and saw me peeking over the banister. "Oh! There you are, Hannah. Come say hello to our next-door neighbor."

I trudged downstairs to meet Rebecca Perfect.

You've got to hand it to Mrs. Perfect: On first impression, she really lives up to her name. She wore a neatly tailored pantsuit, designer shoes with tiny heels, and black leather gloves. Not a hair was out of place. She smiled with approval, as she swiftly eyed me from head-to-toe.

"Hi," I said, extending my hand.

"Does Hannah babysit?" Mrs. Perfect directed her question to my mother as she shook my hand with a limp grip that was more of a pinch than a handshake.

"Oh, yes. Hannah is a very experienced babysitter. Right, Hannah?"

"I'm so glad," said Mrs. Perfect, before I had a chance to answer. "I realize this is a last-minute request, but my husband and I have a very important engagement tonight. Could you come over to our place at about seven o'clock, Hannah?"

"Okay," I said. "But don't your kids go trick-or-treating on Halloween night?"

"They prefer to celebrate the holiday at home."

I'd like to tell you that I had some sense of foreboding about a last-minute babysitting invitation on Halloween night, but I didn't. I was thrilled, even relieved. For one thing, it was nice to have any kind of social invitation in a town where I knew absolutely nobody. Besides, I've always liked kids, probably because children and babies have always been drawn to me. Babies like pulling on my long ponytail and hoop earrings, and older kids like the silly games I make up after their parents leave the house. Back in my old neighborhood I made a small fortune as a babysitter. In fact, when my dad lost his job, he joked that I was going to have to step in as the breadwinner of the family. With no friends in my new neighborhood, I figured I might as well spend Halloween night babysitting.

As I was contemplating my luck at finding a babysitting job so quickly, Mrs. Perfect pulled her cell phone from her purse, opened it, and snapped my picture with a single swift movement. "For my children," she explained, punching a number into her phone with her gloved finger. "So you won't be a complete stranger when you come over."

"Oh. Sure." Nobody had ever taken my picture in advance of a babysitting job before. *Maybe she's actually taking the picture as a security precaution since she doesn't know me well,* I thought.

Well, in hindsight, I know that Mrs. Perfect was telling the truth: The photo really *was* for her kids. Just not in the way I expected.

"So we live next door to the Perfects," I remarked wryly after we said good-bye to our new neighbor. "I guess we're moving up in the world."

"Isn't it funny?!" My mom grabbed a pair of scissors and cut open one of the storage boxes that were stacked in the room. "Here I am looking my worst, and who comes over but 'Mrs. Perfect'!"

Oh, it was funny, all right.

If you like being killed, this whole thing is hilarious.

It's hard to believe that just hours ago, I was sitting on a window seat in my new bedroom peering down into the next-door neighbors' backyard and feeling almost happy as I spied on Mrs. Perfect's three kids—a girl and boy who appeared to be about five or six, and a baby girl who looked as if she were about one year old. The children were cute, but something about their demeanor seemed joyless and somber—older than their years. Sitting silently in an old-fashioned baby buggy, even the baby struck me as unusually reserved and serious as she sucked on her bottle.

Surrounding the children were some of the most enthusiastic backyard Halloween decorations I had ever seen. Tiny ghosts made of gauzy material dangled from tree branches, dancing in the wind. The lawn resembled a tiny church graveyard filled with small, fake tombstones. Well, I assumed they were fake. It's funny how the scene struck me as simultaneously adorable and sad. For some reason, I felt sorry for those strangely forlorn little kids. I imagined myself befriending them: reading funny stories, playing hide-and-seek in the yard, tickling the baby's toes and making her giggle.

I must have dozed off while sitting in the window seat daydreaming, because the next thing I knew, all three children had vanished from the garden below. I felt strangely dizzy, so I decided to take a walk and get some fresh air.

I quickly realized that it took only about ten minutes to see just about everything there was to see in the town of Entrails—a "dollar store," a bakery, a McDonald's, a gas station, a church, a dentist's office, a bar called Tim's Lounge, and a gift shop called Sweet Memories that sold sentimental greeting cards, candles, and hundreds of dolls and stuffed animals dressed up in elaborate costumes. A large, vintage-looking sign on the wall in Sweet Memories announced:

Custom-Built Dolls
⟡ REAL HAIR ⟡
Order Today

I had never seen so much velvet and lace in one store, and I couldn't help wondering how a store that sold mostly dolls could stay in business in such a small town. It was as silent as a tomb in the store; I was the only customer in sight.

As I browsed shelves stacked with floppy-eared rabbits wearing petticoats and dolls with clear-blue glass eyes that stared out of painted porcelain faces, the ladies working at the checkout counter observed me with prim, unfriendly interest. All three were middle-aged, dressed in colorful, preppy sweaters.

"She's the one," I heard one of the ladies whisper.

I felt paranoid. Were they talking about me?

"They already moved into the Morgan house?" The other lady didn't even try to lower her voice.

"Morgan" was the name of the family who used to live in our new house. Now I felt certain they were talking about me.

"I recognize her from the rush order we got in earlier today."

What "rush order"? I wondered. What were they talking about?

"Shame about the Morgans."

"They say one person's misfortune is another's opportunity."

Were they annoyed that my family had snapped up their former neighbor's foreclosed property? It wasn't my family's fault the Morgans couldn't pay their mortgage, was it?

"Shame about that poor girl Jessica, too."

Who in the world was Jessica, and what happened to *her*? Now I was too curious to keep quiet. I figured these ladies knew just about everything that went on in the town of Entrails, so I thought I'd try to talk to them.

"Excuse me," I ventured. "I couldn't help overhearing you. . . . My name is Hannah and my family just moved into the house the Morgans used to own."

The three women stared as if they were shocked that

I knew how to talk. One of them refused to make eye contact: She looked down, pretended to shuffle some papers, then turned and walked away, shaking her head. Was I going to be a social outcast in my new town?

"Um—sorry to interrupt your work," I said, secretly reflecting that they had actually been standing there doing nothing. "I'm just curious about the neighborhood, and I heard you mention something about the Morgans— the people who used to live in our house."

"You don't *know* what happened to the Morgans?" The woman standing at the cash register squinted at me as if trying to see me more clearly.

I shook my head. As far as I knew, my parents didn't know either.

"They had a girl about your age," she said, coldly. "She went missing. Nobody knows *exactly* what happened, but she's gone."

At these words, I felt a cold sensation in my bones, like a warning from my own body. I guess my body was smarter than my brain.

"We can *guess* what happened," the other lady mumbled.

"Carol—" The other lady shot Carol a warning glance, as if telling her to put a lid on it. "You don't want to scare the girl."

"I think she has a right to know *something*." Carol turned

back to me and gave me a pointed look. "Anyway, things have a way of falling apart after something like that."

I already knew we had moved to a small, boring town, but now it seemed that we had moved to a small, *creepy* (not to mention decidedly *unfriendly*) town. What in the world had my parents been thinking?

"So what do you think happened to Jessica?" I asked.

"All we can tell you is that none of the Morgans are around anymore."

"Well, thanks for the info," I said, feeling overwhelmed and suddenly wanting to get out of that store as quickly as possible,

"Just be careful around here," Carol warned.

"I will," I said, not having the faintest idea *how*, exactly, I was supposed to "be careful."

A fall storm was brewing as I approached the Perfects' house in darkness. Dry leaves stirred and whispered in the warm wind reminding me of tornado weather.

"Hello, Hannah." Mrs. Perfect greeted me at the door. Her slender figure was defined by an elegantly tailored black dress, a long strand of pearls, and shiny high heels.

"Thank you for coming over at such short notice." Mrs. Perfect spoke with a cool familiarity, once again eyeing me up and down, as if conducting a quick assessment of my skin, hair, and body. Registering a tiny smile, she stepped aside so I could walk past her. I felt her eyes on me as she followed me into an enormous, high-ceilinged kitchen where two of the children I had observed through the window earlier in the day sat on stools around a high table, eating dinner.

The kids regarded me with mild interest, but without smiling.

"Hannah, these are my children, Maddie and Jackson."

Maddie and Jackson said hello and then turned back to watching a large flat-screen television. I don't think I had ever met anybody whose kitchen contained such a huge flat-screen television.

As I mentioned before, I've always liked children— kids of all ages, sizes, colors, and shapes. In my experience, there's always something funny or cute about even the most difficult or homely child. But strangely, I found myself reflecting that Maddie and Jackson had looked a whole lot cuter from the safe distance of my bedroom window. Up close, something was *wrong* with these two kids. I just couldn't put my finger on what, exactly, it was. Maybe it was the way their blue eyes had a glassy, puffy look that suggested illness. Their rosy, flushed cheeks looked feverish instead of healthy. *Maybe they're fighting a flu bug*, I thought. But then I realized that it wasn't so much their appearance but what they were *doing*—and what they were *watching*—that made these two children instinctively unappealing.

Maddie's and Jackson's sharp knives and forks clinked against their plates as they carved nearly raw slabs of steak, their white porcelain plates stained with bloody juices. While they ate, they calmly watched television footage of a surgical procedure with the volume muted. Chewing their red meat and gulping their milk, they stared as scalpels made incisions and clamps revealed internal organs.

"You like watching this stuff?" I was baffled by the family's choice of viewing material during a meal.

The kids nodded with blank expressions.

I wanted to ask Mrs. Perfect whether her children always watched surgical procedures during meals, but before I could say anything, she placed a piece of paper in front of me—a set of typed, detailed instructions. She would be meeting her husband at a Halloween gathering where she couldn't be reached by phone. Maddie and Jackson were allowed to watch television, followed by an early bedtime. She expected to be back home no later than 10:00 P.M.

"Help yourself to anything you'd like in the kitchen, Hannah," said Mrs. Perfect, opening the refrigerator door to reveal a sparse collection of yogurts and a plate littered with the bones of a small animal that didn't look like anything I had ever eaten before.

"And what about the baby?" I asked. "What's her schedule?"

Mrs. Perfect frowned. "What baby?"

Again, you have to give Mrs. Perfect some credit for playing her role so well. She seemed so genuinely taken aback by my comment, I actually felt embarrassed and a little ashamed for asking it.

"Sorry," I said, "but I thought I saw a baby with Maddie and Jackson in your backyard earlier today."

Out of the corner of my eye, I thought I perceived the faintest twitch of amusement on the meat-stained lips of the children.

"Maybe you saw one of Maddie's dolls," said Mrs. Perfect curtly.

"Wasn't there a baby outside with you guys earlier today?" I turned to Maddie and Jackson. "She was holding a bottle."

Maddie and Jackson stared at me with inscrutable expressions and shook their heads without speaking. Their reluctance to speak annoyed me; it seemed more like an aggressive reluctance than innocent shyness. Moreover, I was bewildered by the contradiction between what I had seen and what Mrs. Perfect was telling me. If Maddie and Jackson were the only children who lived in this house, who was the baby I had seen in their garden? Had I imagined her? Had I seen a ghost?

"Well, I'd better be going," said Mrs. Perfect, throwing a vintage fox wrap around her shoulders that, bizarrely, still had the fox's head attached. "I'll be back by ten o'clock at the latest." She gave Maddie and Jackson a quick peck on the cheek and left without another word.

"So," I said, pulling up a stool to sit next to the children. "What kind of surgery are we watching here?" I did my best to sound friendly and nonchalant—to conceal my squeamishness.

"Appendectomy," muttered Jackson.

"I prefer to watch brain surgery," I joked.

The kids regarded me with surprise, but they didn't laugh. I tried a different approach. "Are you guys interested in becoming surgeons someday?"

Both kids shook their heads. "Our dad used to own a medical devices company," Jackson explained, "but he wasn't a surgeon."

"What kind of devices did his company make?"

"All kinds," said Maddie. "But he sold the company. That's how we got our money."

"I see." I got the impression that quite a lot of money

came from that medical devices company. I doubted I'd be running into the Perfect children working at the Sweet Memories store or the local McDonald's.

"How about some dessert?" I eyed the blobs of bloody juice and fat on the kids' plates, and felt a little unnerved when I noticed that Jackson had apparently eaten part of a bone. I opened a cabinet and was relieved when I saw ordinary, unhealthy snacks: potato chips, Cheetos, Oreo cookies. Not one of the packages had been opened.

"No, thanks," said Maddie. "We just keep those for babysitters."

"Maybe some ice cream?" I pressed. I absentmindedly opened a cabinet door to look for more snacks and discovered the most extensive and elaborate collection of kitchen knives I had ever seen in anyone's house. Was it my imagination, or were there some surgical tools amid the knives, too? I slammed the cabinet door shut.

"I'm saving my appetite for later," said Jackson.

I saw Maddie kick her brother under the table, as if nudging him to be quiet.

After the kids dutifully washed their dishes and put them in the dishwasher, Maddie announced that she was going upstairs to her room to read. This was a little disappointing since kids usually want to spend time with me, but it was clear that she didn't want any company.

There was nothing to do but follow Jackson into the family room.

After watching a surgery in the Perfects' kitchen, I should have been prepared for their living room, but I wasn't. No fewer than three enormous television screens displayed silent, repeating black-and-white film segments of striking violence: a firing squad execution, a cruel animal-testing process in a laboratory, and war footage. The spacious room resembled a disturbing art museum installation. The volume was turned down completely: a silent series of violent actions repeated themselves again and again. Was this some kind of modern art, or was it a Halloween stunt?

Suspended over the fireplace was an enormous portrait of the Perfect family. I examined the picture and realized that it was true: There were only two children— no baby. At least not in the picture.

"Do you want to watch something else?" I asked Jackson, who was now sprawled on a black leather couch. "A movie or something?"

"Nah."

I sat down next to Jackson, doing my best to bond with him. But while the silent images on the screen seemed to relax Jackson, they made me feel overwhelmingly anxious. More than anything, I felt the urge to flee the house. And once again, my body was smarter than my brain.

Hannah . . .

I heard the faint sound of someone calling my name.

"Was that Maddie?" I asked.

"I didn't hear anything." Jackson stared at the black-and-white images flickering across the television screens.

"I'll just go check on her."

I made my way upstairs then down a hallway decorated with a bizarre combination of technology, weaponry, and sentimental whimsy. Artifacts including swords and antique rifles were displayed alongside sappy oil paintings depicting lush flower gardens, waterfalls, and sunsets. I found one object particularly disturbing—a large, Victorian-style wreath that appeared at first glance to be an intricate arrangement of dried flowers. When I took a closer look, I realized that the brown and gold petals and leaves were actually made entirely of human *hair*—hair of various shades that had been braided and twisted into detailed shapes. Was this evidence of some bizarre family hobby? *And whose hair was it?*

Now opening a series of doors in search of Maddie's bedroom, I had the disconcerting sense that it was entirely possible to lose track of a child in this house. Who knew how many hiding places there were—how many secret rooms?

"Maddie!" I called.

The only answer was a thin, wailing sound like the whistling of wind around a house or the plaintive meow of a cat. As I listened more closely, I became convinced that it was the sound of a baby crying.

I hurried up another flight of stairs. The crying seemed to come from behind a closed door at the end of another long hallway.

I caught my breath when I pulled open the door to reveal a baby's nursery. My eyes fell on a small, empty bassinet adorned with a skirt of white lace. All around the bed were dolls dressed in clothing from various historical eras: hoop skirts made of colorful taffeta; wasp-waisted polka-dot dresses with crinoline petticoats; miniskirts and go-go boots. My interest in the elaborate and intricate costumes worn by these dolls turned to trepidation when I noticed a group of dolls that looked like ordinary, contemporary teenagers—dolls dressed in blue jeans, dolls carrying tiny backpacks and miniature cell phones. One even had braces painted on small, plastic teeth.

I wanted to examine the dolls more closely, but the cries of the phantom baby were becoming evermore insistent. Strangely, the infant's screaming now seemed to come from behind a full-length mirror that hung on the wall.

Now I know where that old saying "curiosity killed the cat" comes from. It's funny how you can feel simultaneously terrified and driven to discover the truth at all costs. Well, that's how I felt as I slowly approached my own reflection in the mirror, bracing myself for the glimpse of some supernatural vision in the darkened glass.

I reached out and touched my reflection and gasped with surprise when the mirror quietly swung open to reveal a tiny room.

The mirror was actually a secret doorway. There, behind the mirror, was the source of the crying: a baby monitor with a video screen. I had used plenty of baby monitors, so I knew they were basically walkie-talkies that allowed you to hear and even see a baby from any room in the house. Now I knew for sure that there really *was* a baby—the same baby girl I had seen in the garden earlier that day. Wearing only a diaper, she sat alone in what looked like an animal cage. I watched the grainy image on the screen as she pulled herself up to a standing position and stood with one arm outstretched through the bars of her little prison.

"Mama!" she cried.

My stomach churned when I perceived a tiny, grue-some detail—the shadowy image of a butcher knife lying on the floor near the baby.

Someone wants me to see this, I thought. *But why?* I remembered Maddie kicking Jackson under the table, the sly smile on Jackson's lips when I had asked about a baby.

I was sure of one thing: I had to find that baby. In the background of the image on the video screen I saw the outline of what looked like a wine storage cabinet. My gut told me that the baby was somewhere in the basement of the house.

In retrospect, going down to the basement by myself wasn't a good idea. But something takes over when you see and hear a child in distress: It's almost a full-body alarm that compels you to act without thinking, to run as fast as you can toward the sobbing sounds. At least that's how it was for me.

As I raced down a series of stairways and then through the family room, where the disturbing screen images were still looping, I heard the patter of rain outside the window—a fall storm beginning. As a flash of lightning illuminated the Halloween cemetery in the backyard, I remembered the story of the teenage girl named Jessica who had disappeared. *How many kids are buried back there?* I wondered. *How many families?*

I made my way through a library (where I glimpsed a book entitled *Best Meat-Carving Methods*) then through a game room and a reading alcove, then down the steep, dark steps leading to the Perfects' basement.

I could hear the crying more clearly now, but it sounded softer, as if the child had grown weary.

"Hello? Is anybody here?"

Across the dim room I saw the dark outline of the cage. Something sat inside: the motionless shadow-silhouette of a child. Was she okay? Had she been hurt?

I cautiously approached the cage until I was close enough to see clearly in the dim light.

The cage door was open and there was no baby. Instead, there was a large doll—*a doll that bore a striking resemblance to me.* I stared for a moment too long, horrified and mesmerized by the doll's hoop earrings—the long, shiny hair gathered in a ponytail. Several hands shoved me from behind.

I toppled into the cage and the door slammed behind me.

When I turned around and caught my breath, I saw the whole Perfect family—including a very familiar one-year-old baby and two of the middle-aged ladies from the Sweet Memories shop—hugging each other, pulling out their carving knives, and wishing each other a happy Halloween.

"My parents know where I am!" I shouted, my voice sounding strangely hollow. "My dad will make sure you all go to jail forever!"

"Things don't work that way around here, dear," said Mrs. Perfect calmly. "You see, we Perfects pretty much keep this town running. We have an arrangement with the townsfolk. We stay away from the kids who were born and raised here, and help keep their businesses afloat, and they keep their noses out of our culinary activities. Let's just say the police won't be terribly concerned when they hear you're missing."

"Still, you won't get away with this." I realized I was speaking to someone who had absolute certainty that she *would* indeed get away with it forever.

"You'd be shocked at how many parents can be bought," said Mrs. Perfect. "Just say the words 'financial security' and 'never have to work again' and some of them are willing to keep quiet. Others—well, we have ways of keeping them quiet."

So there you have it. In the town of Entrails, the Perfect family keeps the town running financially and, in exchange, the townsfolk and the police keep quiet about their crimes. In a sense, my family really did move next door to a castle; the whole thing is kind of feudal. If I were going to school again, I'd write a paper about it.

But don't worry. I haven't given up all hope yet. Remember how I said kids always like me? Well, toddlers *love* me. And just a moment ago, after all the other Perfects disappeared to go sharpen their knives and fingernails in preparation for their Halloween feast of freshly killed babysitter, the littlest Perfect appeared outside my cage with an impish, toothy grin and a shiny key in her hand. Maybe—just maybe—she'll trade the key to the cage for the doll that looks like me.

Kids. You never know what they're going to do.

SHADOW CHILDREN

· HEATHER BREWER ·

"ood night, Jon." Dax pulled the covers over his little brother's chest. Jon was wearing his favorite pajamas again, despite the hour-long argument that flannel wasn't exactly a summer-weight fabric and the buttons were on the verge of falling off. Surrendering with a sigh, Dax walked out of the room, flipping the light switch as he went. Not a second later, Jon's Batman night-light went out, which instantly sparked whining from the six-year-old.

"Dax, my night-light! I can't sleep without my night-light. The shadows will get me!"

Dax sighed again, silently counting the seconds until Mom and Dad would be home. It was like this every night. John would whine to Mom or Dad and they'd make sure his night-light was working or that the hall light was on, anything to placate Jon's irrational fear of things that weren't really lurking in the shadows, waiting to snatch him away. Only tonight, it was Dax who was left to placate him. Bad enough he had to miss out on Janie's party to babysit his little brother, but now he was also expected to cater to Jon's ridiculous fear of the dark. "I'll grab you a flashlight, Jon. Just give me a second."

It was all he could do to block out Jon's blubbering as he walked into the kitchen. He pulled the drawer open and rummaged around. A flashlight had to be in there somewhere.

"Dax, hurry! The shadows!"

Dax found a couple of flashlights and picked one up, tapping it gently against his chin. Maybe it would be better if he did them all a favor and showed Jon that there were no such things as monsters under your bed, nothing at all lurking in the pitch-black night. If he let Jon cry it out just for one night, maybe the kid would grow up and stop being such a baby. Maybe then babysitting him without pay and missing out on the party of the year wouldn't be so bad. Dax mulled this over for a moment, blocking out the whimpers from down the hall. "It's just the dark, Jon. There's nothing in it that isn't there in the daytime."

Jon screamed. And it wasn't one of those little-brat screams for attention. He sounded terrified. Like his life depended on someone hearing and responding to his terrified shriek.

Dax bolted back to the bedroom and stared in shocked disbelief.

A long, dark shadow was looming over the bed. But it wasn't an ordinary shadow. It was darker than the rest of the room, and moved of its own free will. It was a creature made of shadows. It was alive. Part of it whipped forward and wrapped around Jon's ankle. Jon cried, "Help me, Dax!"

The shadow monster was pulling Jon off the bed, but Dax was frozen in place, staring at this thing that couldn't possibly exist. Jon was flailing, tears streaming down his cheeks. Breaking free from his trance, Dax clutched his brother's wrist, but he was hit in the chest and thrown against the wall. Pain bolted through Dax's back as he hit the wall and crumpled to the floor. He struggled to sit up again, but a tentacle of the shadow monster stood in front of him, defying him to move. There were no eyes or mouth, but somehow Dax knew that the thing was looking at him. He swore he heard a growl, but it had no mouth, no substance. The shadow monster lurched back and ripped Dax's brother free of his covers.

Dax ran forward and grabbed Jon by the ankle. They both flew through the air and into the closet. The door slammed shut, sealing them in pitch-black.

A sound caught his attention, like a large amount of sand falling through a grainy hourglass. It was coming from the floor. Dax looked down. The floor was moving. It swirled around his feet; the sandlike substance of what had once been a wood floor crashed over the toe of his sock in small, black waves. He pulled his foot back, but the sand clung to it. Beside him, Jon whimpered as the sand closed over his arm. Dax brushed it away, but it seemed to have a life of its own. The sand covered him, and all he could do was lie there, feeling the weight of it curl around his feet, his ankles, his legs, knowing he was sinking into it—whatever it was. It moved up his torso, and he felt suffocated. There was no air, only sand.

Beside him, Jon screamed, but his screams were cut off as the sand closed over his small head. Dax grabbed desperately for Jon's hand, but there was nothing to grab. His brother was gone.

Strangely, he could feel his legs dangling on the other side, like he was slipping through some hole. It covered his chest and Dax took a deep breath and held it, not knowing if he would ever breathe again, not knowing what was happening or what to do to stop it. The sand swirled around, tickling his eyelashes, covering his face. He felt the weight of it on top of his head, and wondered if he would ever see Jon again.

Suddenly, the sand impacted tightly around him and, just as quickly, released. Dax fell several feet, landing on the hard ground below. He coughed and drew air into his lungs. His chest burned, but after a few deep breaths, it came easy again. Remembering the flashlight, he turned it on and looked around, gasping at what he saw.

He was in a cavern. An enormous cavern of what must have been obsidian—the walls were shiny and black, the floor smooth and reflective. He shined the flashlight up at where he'd fallen through, but there was no sign of any hole or trapdoor, or even sand. Only hard, black rock. The floor trembled slightly beneath his feet. He noticed the movement less when he stepped forward, but despite the floor's solid appearance, it struck him as fragile.

On the ceiling, just on the edge of the flashlight beam, something moved. Dax chased it with the light, but it remained at the beam's edge. And like that, on the edge of his hearing, Dax detected a sound, like a group of people whispering very softly. "Hello?"

In the distance, a noise. It sounded like his brother crying.

"Jon? Where are you?" But silence answered him. Dax called out again, but the only sound was his voice chasing after itself in an echo.

The last thing he wanted to do was move deeper into the cavernous tunnel, to move away from this spot, which he feared was the closest he would ever be to home again, but Jon had sounded like he was getting farther and farther away, so he had no choice. He had to find his brother, and then, he had to find a way to get them out of here.

Clutching the flashlight in his hand, Dax moved through the cavern. All around him he could hear faint whispers but couldn't understand what they were saying. He paused several times, shining the light behind him, trying to catch whoever—whatever—was whispering, but each and every time there was no one there. Dax was, despite the nudging of the darkest corners of his imagination, completely alone.

Jon was nowhere to be found. It was as if he'd vanished into thin air.

The large tunnel broke off into three smaller tunnels up ahead. Dax listened, but heard nothing that told him which one Jon might be down. He ran a frustrated hand through his hair and, just as he'd decided to take the middle tunnel, the whispering stopped and a new sound began. A small click as something hit the floor, then an even smaller noise, like something rolling several feet. He pointed the flashlight down, searching, sweeping the floor for any sign of movement. The sound ceased as whatever it was rattled to a stop just in front of his feet. He bent down, focusing on the item with the light. In near disbelief, he plucked it from the ground, turning it over in his hand.

A red, shiny button. Just like the ones on Jon's pajamas.

Dax stood, shining the flashlight on the tunnels again. "Jon?"

He stepped forward and, just as he was about to enter the center tunnel, he saw movement with his peripheral vision. Taking a step back, he shined his light on the right tunnel entrance. At first there was nothing, but after a moment, Dax thought he could hear a small whimper. He hurried down the right tunnel, clutching the button in his hand and calling out for his brother.

Several yards in, the whispers returned, but though they were louder in the smaller space, Dax still couldn't determine where they were coming from or what they were saying. It was unnerving, as though he were being followed by someone without a voice, who insisted on making themselves known. His flashlight flickered and went out. The whispers grew louder and felt as if they were closing in, but that was crazy. They were just noises . . . weren't they? Dax knocked the light against his palm. When the flickering subsided and the light returned, the whispers ceased . . . and someone was standing in the tunnel with him.

He would have recognized that face and those pajamas anywhere. Relieved to see his brother again, he stepped forward. "There you are. I've been looking everywh—"

The child had his arm extended, stroking the walls in a loving manner that sent a chill up Dax's spine. Something about the way he moved seemed unnatural. Suddenly, but calmly, he turned his head toward Dax. Dax's trembling fingers found his open mouth, hushing a gasp. The child had Jon's mouth, his cheeks, his forehead, his hair, but the eyes . . . they were filled with shadows.

The thing in front of him might have looked like Jon, but it wasn't his brother. It was something else. Something sinister. Something dark.

Dax backed up, clutching the flashlight tightly to his chest. When he hit the tunnel wall, he expected it to be cool, but it was warm, almost like a living entity. Even though he knew that it wasn't Jon, he swallowed hard and whispered his brother's name.

The Jon-thing turned slowly, without speaking, and disappeared around the bend.

Dax's heart slammed against his ribs. His breath came in quick gasps. Panic overtook him, but he forced himself to move forward, because something inside of him told him that the Jon-thing knew where his real brother was. Dax turned around the bend, reluctantly following wherever it was that the Jon-thing was leading.

By the time he turned the corner, it was already moving around the next bend. Dax picked up the pace, jogging after the thing that looked like his brother.

After several more bends in the tunnel, he turned a corner into a small room. A boy was lying on the floor in the fetal position, shuddering with sobs. Raising every hair on the back of Dax's neck, the Jon-thing bent down and stroked the boy's hair wordlessly with its small, pale fingers. The boy scrambled away from him, terrified, and Dax shot forward, hugging his brother—his actual brother—tightly. At first, Jon screamed and pushed him away, but then, realizing that it was Dax, he clung to his brother's chest, sobbing into his shirt, soaking the fabric. "It's okay," Dax whispered into his hair, not entirely certain he was telling his brother the truth. "It's going to be okay."

The Jon-thing tilted its head. When it spoke its voice mimicked Jon's perfectly, but still something seemed off about it, false. "You shouldn't lie to children."

Dax sneered. "What are you?"

It smiled, its dry, cracking lips stretching back from its Jon-like teeth, which seemed sharper than Jon's, hungrier. "We are shadow children."

Instinctively, Dax looked around, but saw no one else. "We?"

The Jon-thing smiled and looked up, as if exchanging bemused glances with someone that Dax couldn't see. "We tire of the darkness. We want to live as you live."

A small trail of colored dust, shimmering and full of light, floated in the air between Jon and the monster that was mimicking his form. Jon swooned, not at all steady on his feet. He looked pale. He looked weak. The sickening realization hit Dax that the creature was somehow feeding on his brother, sucking his essence from him and stealing his shape. Maybe it was the only way the thing could become solid. Maybe without whatever it was that it was stealing from Jon it couldn't become anything more than the horrible shadow that had snatched Jon from his bed. Maybe it couldn't face the light before and somehow Jon knew that, and when Dax had forced his brother to remain in the darkness . . .

Dax swallowed the lump in his throat. It didn't go down easily.

It was his fault. Jon knew that these things existed, and he knew how to keep them at bay. Dax ignored that, brushing it off as just a stupid little-kid fear, and let the monsters in.

It stretched out its hand again, caressing Jon's hair the way someone might pet a puppy. Dax jerked Jon from it and glared. It met his gaze with its shadowy eyes, blinking like it couldn't possibly understand why he wouldn't want it touching his brother. "You cannot escape."

Dax gripped Jon to him, standing, holding his brother as tightly as he could without hurting him. He looked at the Jon-thing and tightened his jaw. "Watch me."

With Jon in his arms, he bolted back down the tunnel, back the way he'd come. As he ran, the indistinguishable whispers started again, quickly growing louder until they were almost deafening. Jon cried against his chest, so scared of what was happening, and Dax ran as fast as he could, darting around corners with ease. The whispers grew faint as he ran. He was beating them, beating them all. Finally, out of breath and with nowhere else to run, he entered the large cavern that they had first fallen

into. Dax sat Jon down on the ground, only then noticing that the trail of shimmering dust still hung in the air,
winding its way through the tunnels. Running from the
Jon-thing wasn't enough to sever that essence-stealing
tie. His brother tugged at his sleeve, still trembling, but
Dax was firm. "Hold on, Jon. Let me figure this out."

On the ceiling, just on the edge of the flashlight beam,
something moved.

Dax chased it with the light, but it remained at the
beam's edge, just as before. Then suddenly, his ears were
filled with a thousand whispery, deafening sounds. He
waved the flashlight around, and terror filled him.

Strange shadow creatures, like the monster that had
grabbed Jon from his bed, peeled from the cave's ceiling, from its walls and floor. One flew dangerously close
to Dax and he ducked back, but not before seeing the
image of a young girl's face reflected in its shadowy
substance. The sight of it startled him. It wasn't just
Jon that they were after. They flew from their place in
the cave and swirled around the two boys, surrounding
them completely, blocking any chance of escape. Each
of the shadows wore the face of a child; some Dax knew
personally. The Jon-thing had said that they tired of the
darkness, that they wanted what Dax and Jon had, what

everybody had. The creatures were going to make mirror forms of every kid on earth, and then what? Kill them all? Suck them dry of their essence, leaving them empty, hollow shells? Panic set in and Dax gasped for air. Layers and layers of the cave floor and walls peeled away until Dax could see what they were peeling away from—and it wasn't black rock. With horrified understanding, he realized that there was no cave. The creatures *were* the cave.

Thousands, maybe millions, of shadow monsters out to replace the people of the world. Dax's heart raced. Beside him, Jon screamed as the shadows closed in.

The floor shrank until there was only an island of shadow left. It trembled wildly beneath their feet.

Dax whipped his flashlight around in desperation. On a low part of the cave ceiling, he saw a flash of color, something brown and familiar.

He scooped Jon up in his arms and said, "Hold on tight."

One of the shadows whipped forward, snatching the flashlight from Dax's grip. It threw the light down, smashing it to bits, leaving them all in darkness. The shadow monsters swarmed closer to the boys, and just as a long shadowy tentacle reached for Jon, Dax leaped toward the familiar sight on the low cave ceiling and clung to the hole in the floor of Jon's closet with the tips of his deter-mined fingers. His biceps burned, but he pulled himself up until he was waist-high into the closet. "Jon, get off now! I'm falling!"

Jon scrambled from his brother through his pitch-black room to his bed, drenched in sweat and tears, cry-ing for his brother to hurry, hurry before those monsters got him.

Something wrapped around Dax's ankle and pulled hard; it was no use. It pulled him back down into the cave, the tips of his fingers only barely clinging to the wood.

He was going to fall. And once he did, those things would suck every bit of his essence away.

A beam of light suddenly shined down into the hole and the creatures backed off. Dax looked up. Jon was holding a flashlight he must have retrieved from the kitchen. Dax pulled himself free from the hole, his muscles burning. He collapsed onto the floor of Jon's closet and hugged his brother, trying to stanch his tears, but the danger wasn't over. There was still a hole in the closet floor. It was still dark.

Whispers drifted up from the hole until they were fill-ing the room. Jon's flashlight flickered out, as if it couldn't stand up against the growing darkness. Dax picked up his brother and ran for the door. They had to get out of there, away from the darkness, into the light.

The bedroom door opened and their mother flipped the light switch, bathing the room in incandescent light. "Where have you boys been?! Your father and I have been worried sick!"

Dax panted, his heart settling into a more normal rhythm. He looked at the closet, at the perfect, unbroken floor. Jon ran across the room and jumped into his mother's arms. Dax couldn't help but notice that the trail of dust was gone, the Jon-thing's connection to him broken at last.

Holding Jon, placing kisses on his cheeks, their mom crossed the room and opened the heavy drapes, letting sunlight inside. It was morning. Had they really been gone that long? It had felt like minutes, maybe an hour, but certainly not several hours.

She turned back to Dax with a concerned look on her face. "Dax? Is everything okay? We were so scared that something happened to you both."

Dax slowly nodded his head, even though everything was about as far from okay as it could get, and looked from the closet to the sunny day outside. Out the window, he could see the neighbor kids playing soccer. To any onlooker, it would seem like an ordinary, normal day.

He turned back to his mom and released a relieved sigh. "Yeah, Mom. Everything's fine. We just—"

As she turned around, Jon peered over his mother's shoulder at Dax, who froze. Jon smiled and offered a wave.

Shadows lurked in his eyes—the darkest that Dax had ever seen.

THE POISON RING

· PEG KEHRET ·

The antiques business was fun until the burglaries began. After school and on Saturdays, I work at my mom's store, Off-Line Antiques. When I arrived last Friday, Mom said, "Someone burglarized Rosie's Posies and the theater last night. They took Rosie's computer, cases of candy from the theater, and cash from both places."

Claire, a teller at the corner bank, came in on her break. After we discussed the burglaries, Claire said, "You called about a cat ring?" She collects cat items, so Mom alerts her when we have something she might want.

Mom handed the ring to Claire. The top of the ring

was an oval-shaped tile, with a black-and-white cat painted on it. "It's a poison ring," Mom said, "circa 1820."

Claire looked up. "Poison?"

"See the hidden clasp? It opens." Mom demonstrated how the top of the ring lifted up, revealing a secret compartment. "The rings were made to hide poison," Mom said, "although they were often used to carry a loved one's lock of hair."

"How much is it?"

She and Mom settled on a price, and Claire wore the ring back to work.

A frail white-haired woman carrying a faded paisley tote bag came in.

"What did you bring today, Mrs. Pameron?" Mom asked.

"More things from Maud." She removed a brass candlestick from the bag, followed by a stained rag doll that was missing half her hair. When Mrs. Pameron had first come to the shop, months earlier, she had brought treasured keepsakes. Her eyes often filled with tears as she told where she and her late husband had purchased a particular item. Every piece she brought had a history, and Mom bought them all.

After a while, her personal stories stopped and she

began selling us her sister's belongings. The quality of the goods gradually got worse, but Mom still purchased some items from Mrs. Pameron because she felt sorry for her. The woman always wore the same frayed sweater, and she had memory problems. "She probably needs the money," Mom said.

Mrs. Pameron took an old tin Santa out of her bag. "I'll take the Santa," Mom said, "but not the rest. The candlestick isn't old, and the doll is in poor condition."

"I'll be back tomorrow," Mrs. Pameron said as Mom paid for the Santa. "This was all I could carry."

"I could go to your sister's house," Mom said, "and buy what I can use."

"You can't do that," Mrs. Pameron said. "Oh, no. You mustn't do that."

When we left that day, we double-checked the doors to be sure they were locked, but we still felt uneasy knowing that a burglar had struck so close by. We considered spending the night in the shop, but Mom decided we couldn't let fear rule our lives.

The next morning we got more bad news. The bank where Claire works had been robbed at closing time the night before. The robber took a bag of money as well as cash and jewelry from customers and bank personnel. A teller pushed a hidden alarm, but the police arrived after the robber had fled. Surveillance video of the suspect in a ski mask and black coat was hazy.

Claire stopped in on her lunch hour. "It was awful," she said. "He only got fifteen dollars in cash from me, but he took my grandmother's watch and the cat ring that I bought from you." She paused a moment, then added, "It was horrible to see that gun pointed at me. I could see the cold look in his eyes, and I knew he would pull the trigger if anyone refused to cooperate."

I shuddered, imagining the scene.

Mrs. Pameron came again on Monday. When she removed a pearl necklace from her bag, Mom said, "Tell me about your sister."

"Maud was the oldest, then Jimmy, then me. Now I'm the only one left."

I blurted out, "Your sister died?"

"Oh, yes, dear," Mrs. Pameron said. "Maud's been gone ten years."

Mom and I glanced at each other. Mrs. Pameron didn't remember telling us that she was selling her sister's items because Maud planned to move. Mom said, "I can't buy from you for a while. I'm sorry. I need to sell some merchandise before I add any more."

Mrs. Pameron gasped and put one hand over her mouth. Her eyes darted toward the door, as if she feared someone might hear our conversation. "But what will I do?" she asked.

"If you need money for living expenses," Mom said, "there are agencies who will help you. Why don't you give me your phone number?"

"I'm not staying at home now. I—I don't have a telephone."

After she left Mom said, "I hated to do that but I don't like to buy items unless I know where they came from."

"If her sister's been dead for ten years," I said, "where did she get the stuff she brought in?"

"Exactly. If it was her own, she wouldn't need to lie."

Mom had a dentist appointment Tuesday, so I was alone in the shop when a young man entered. "Let me talk to the owner," he said.

"She isn't here," I said. "I could have her call you when she gets back."

"Give her a message," he said. "Tell her I don't appreciate the way she treated my aunt."

"Your aunt?"

"Aunt Martha brought antiques to sell and she was turned away."

"You're Mrs. Pameron's nephew?" I asked.

He seemed surprised that I knew the name.

"Mom has bought a lot of items from her," I said, "but we're overstocked now."

He picked up a glass toothpick holder and turned it over to see the price. "You and your mother offer junk store prices to an old woman who isn't right in the head, and then you call them valuable antiques and jack up the price."

I wanted to protest but decided I shouldn't argue with him. He seemed jumpy, and angry. I wondered if he was on drugs.

His gaze swept around the shop. "What a scam!" He threw the toothpick holder to the floor, where it shattered.

"Hey!" I said. "You'll have to pay for that!" But he had already stormed out, leaving the door open.

My hands shook as I closed the door and swept up the broken glass.

When Mom returned, we debated whether or not to tell the police about the incident. We decided not to, knowing it would be my word against the nephew's, who would probably insist the broken toothpick holder was an accident.

I was in class the next morning when Mom's friend

Susan came to get me. "Someone broke into Off-Line Antiques last night," she said as she drove me to the shop. "Nothing was stolen, but the shop was trashed."

Mom was talking to a police officer when I arrived. "We took the cash box and my laptop home last night," she told him. "We thought those were the only items of ours that a thief would want."

WARNING had been spray-painted on a glass display cabinet, and a beautiful carved grandfather's clock had been tipped over so that it crashed into a shelf of fine china, breaking not only the clock but dozens of old Haviland and Wedgwood plates. An oak table that displayed Red Wing pottery had been overturned. Vintage postcards that Mom had carefully sorted by topic were in a heap on the floor.

"It was probably the same person who robbed the flower shop, the theater, and the bank," the officer said. "Maybe he vandalized the store because he was angry when he didn't find cash or any items that are easily sold on the street. Are you insured?"

"Yes, but most antiques are irreplaceable."

"Have you had a problem with any customer recently? Is there someone who has a grudge against you?"

I told him about Mrs. Pameron's nephew. "I don't know his name," I said.

"We'll look into it," the officer said.

Instead of going back to school, I helped Mom clean up the mess. After we swept up the broken china and hauled the clock pieces to the Dumpster in the alley, I felt antsy. At two thirty Mom said it was okay for me to leave. I needed to buy a notebook and some art supplies for a school project.

After I did my shopping, I got in line at Starbucks. When the young woman ahead of me reached for her change, I saw the cat ring on her finger!

I told myself not to jump to conclusions. Many antiques are reproduced. Cheap imitations of poison rings are probably being cranked out in China and imported by the hundreds. I needed a closer look.

As the woman collected her coffee, I stepped out of line so I could watch her. She was alone. When she set her coffee down to add cream to it, I stood beside her and reached for a napkin. As she stirred cream into her coffee, I studied the ring. The band had the burnished patina of old gold, and fine age lines were visible in the painted tile. I clearly saw the small clasp on the side, where the lid opened. It was an antique poison ring with a cat painted on the tile, and I was sure it belonged to Claire.

When the woman left Starbucks I followed, staying near other shoppers so she wouldn't notice me. I hoped to get the license plate number of her car. I removed my cell phone from my backpack and slipped it into my pocket, where I could grab it quickly to call the police. The bank robber had been a man, but this woman probably knew who he was.

She broke into a run, waving at a city bus. As she boarded, I raced forward. The driver waited for me. I walked to a seat in the back, where I could watch the woman.

We rode for ten minutes before she got off. I was afraid I would be too obvious if I exited with her, so I stayed on the bus and watched to see where she went. The woman entered a small brick apartment building. I got out at the next corner and walked back. The sign on the building said SERENE HOMES FOR SENIORS.

She must be visiting someone. Well, it was still a clue. The police could talk to the residents and learn who had company today.

I went inside. A row of mailboxes, with apartment numbers and the names of residents on them, lined one wall. I began copying the names into my notebook. I had written down about half of the names when the door to the closest apartment opened.

I looked up, and froze. Mrs. Pameron's nephew stared at me.

"What are you doing here?" he asked.

"I'm working on a school project," I said. "I have to interview someone who remembers World War II."

He came forward and stood beside me. "You came to talk to Aunt Martha."

"She lives here? I didn't know that!"

"Go inside." He pointed toward the open apartment door.

I backed away from him, toward the outside door. "I need to get home," I said.

"You aren't going anywhere." He grabbed my arm and jerked me toward the room.

"Help!" I yelled.

He yanked harder, shoved me inside the apartment, and slammed the door. He turned a dead-bolt lock.

The woman I had followed was sitting on a sofa, watching *Oprah* and eating a candy bar. Mrs. Pameron sat at a round dining table. She smiled when she saw me. "Hello, dear," she said, as if I visited regularly.

The young woman muted the TV and looked at me. "Who's she?" she asked.

"Her mother owns one of the stores that buy antiques from Aunt Martha."

One of the stores? Mrs. Pameron sells to other shops besides ours? Mom would be interested in that piece of news.

"I saw her in Starbucks," the woman said, "and on the bus."

"I knew it! She followed you! She suspects us, Britney."

The woman turned off the TV. "How could she suspect anything?" she asked.

"Why else would she follow you here?"

"Suspects you of what?" I said.

"It was her," Britney said, pointing at Mrs. Pameron. "She told!" She raised her hand as if to slap Mrs. Pameron.

The old woman cringed.

"No!" I cried. "She didn't tell me anything. I don't know what you're talking about."

Britney lowered her hand.

"Regardless of how much she knows," the man said, "this changes the plan. We need to rob the other bank and leave town today. Now."

"What about the girl?"

"We'll take her along. As soon as we do the bank, we'll get rid of her."

"Get rid of her now, Todd." Britney's voice was like ice.

"There are too many people close by. Even the old duffers in this building would hear a gunshot."

"Help!" I yelled. I tried again to reach the door. "Help me!"

Todd grabbed a dish towel and gagged me with it. I kicked at him. He held my hands behind my back while Britney cut the TV cord and used it to bind my hands.

"What are you doing to Maud?" Mrs. Pameron asked.

"It's a game, Aunt Martha. You're going to play, too." The man tied her hands to the chair back with the lamp cord.

"I don't like this game," Mrs. Pameron said.

Britney removed a wad of money from Mrs. Pameron's bag.

"That's my share," Mrs. Pameron said. "You put that back!"

Britney stuffed the cash in her purse.

Todd put on a long black coat.

"Where are you going?" Mrs. Pameron asked.

"To your house," he said.

"I want to go, too," she said.

No, you don't, I thought. *And neither do I.*

Britney opened the door and peered into the hallway. "All clear," she said.

"I'm right behind you with the gun," Todd told me, "so don't try anything."

Please, I thought. *Please, somebody see me!* But the other apartment doors remained closed.

We walked to a parked white car. Todd opened the back door, and I got in.

"Lie down," Britney said.

I did.

Todd got in the front passenger's seat, and she slid behind the wheel.

I lay on my side, facing the front seat. I twisted my hands back and forth, back and forth, trying to loosen the cord. The movement soon chafed my wrists, but I kept trying.

When the car stopped, Todd pulled a black ski mask over his face.

"Maybe I should keep the gun," Britney said, "to control the girl."

"I'm not going in there unarmed," he said.

Britney looked over her shoulder at me.

I held still.

"You can always use your knife," he said.

They both looked out the window. "Now," she said.

He got out.

She twisted in her seat, watching me. I lay motionless. I knew if she caught me trying to get my hands untied, she'd make sure it didn't happen.

Five minutes later, the front door opened and Todd leaped in. "Got it!" he said.

Britney floored the accelerator, and the car shot forward. The tires squealed as she took a corner too fast. A horn honked.

I twisted my hands frantically.

"There were only two customers," Todd said as he removed the mask, "and they both dropped to the floor as soon as I told them to. The teller was terrified. When I showed her the note, she handed over a bag of bills."

Neither of them paid any attention to me. I squeezed my fingers together, making my hands as small as I could. The knot loosened slightly—just enough for me to free my hands.

I slid my right hand into my pocket and opened my phone. I couldn't call with a gag in my mouth, but I could send a text message. I found the *center* key with my index finger, then slid my finger to the left and pressed. I visualized the keyboard and typed *help*. Next I typed *bnk rbr*. Last, I typed *mrs pam nefw*.

I pressed *center* again. I knew this brought up my list of phone numbers. Mom was first on the list, so I hit *center* again to send my message to her.

I looked out the window, hoping to recognize a landmark so that I could tell Mom where I was. I saw only a stoplight.

"Stay green, baby. Stay green," Todd said. We roared through the intersection. I kept watching. When I spotted the tips of two golden arches, I sent *McD.*

Next I saw the red-and-white logo of the Target store, and texted *trgt.*

"Nobody behind us," Todd said. "No lights, no sirens."

"We did it!" Britney said.

A few minutes later Todd said, "Left at the next corner, where the sign says 'Lake Elgin'. Aunt Martha's house is in about two miles."

Two miles! That didn't give the police enough time to find me.

Panic rose in my throat. I remembered Todd's words: *We'll get rid of her after we rob the bank.*

Soon Todd said, "It's the gravel driveway on the right. Park down by the dock."

The car slowed. The bumpy road curved several times.

"Let's shoot her in the car and push it into the water," Britney said. "We'll be rid of the girl and the getaway car at the same time."

"Hey, this is a good car. We'll shoot her and dump the body off the dock."

I couldn't believe how calmly they discussed my murder. Had they killed before?

The car stopped. "Let's get it over with," Todd said.

They both got out. I slipped my hands back into the knotted cord. I needed more time. I had to stall.

Britney opened the back door. "Out," she said.

"Mmmm," I said as I got out. "Mmmm!"

"Ungag her," Todd said. "No one can hear her yell now."

Britney took the dish towel out of my mouth.

"When your aunt dies, you'll inherit this house," I said.

"What?" said Todd.

"She put it in her will."

"What about her daughter?"

"She said you visit her, and she wants you to have everything."

Britney looked at the classic old house, the wide lawn, and the lake view. "This place is worth a fortune," she said.

"When did my aunt discuss her affairs with you?" Todd asked.

"Sometimes she has tea with Mom and me. One day she asked Mom to recommend an attorney because she wanted to rewrite her will. Mom's brother is a lawyer, and he handled it."

Todd hung on every word, believing my lies. "Where is this new will?" he asked.

"My uncle has the original. He was afraid your aunt

would lose her copy, so Mom kept it at the shop. If you take me there, I'll show it to you."

"She's trying to trick you into taking her home," Britney said.

"Uncle Zach estimated the value of Mrs. Pameron's estate at eight hundred and fifty thousand dollars," I said. "She's leaving it all to you."

Todd's jaw dropped. "Forget Phoenix," he said. "We should stay here and be nice to Aunt Martha."

"She could live another twenty years," Britney said.

"Unless we help her along," Todd said. "She takes a dozen pills every day. It would be easy to overdose on the wrong combination."

He said it as nonchalantly as if he were discussing what to have for dinner.

Britney looked at the house again. "It gets too hot in Phoenix," she said.

"We need to get that will. Then we'll go to Auntie's apartment and help her take her medicine."

An ancient Ford was parked next to the house. "We'll take Aunt Martha's car," Todd said, "in case the cops are looking for mine. She leaves the keys in it."

This time Todd drove.

After I lay down on the backseat, I peeked at my

phone, hoping to see a message from Mom saying that help was on the way.

The phone was dark. My battery needed to recharge. My texts had never been sent.

Fear and despair washed over me. As soon as Todd and Britney realized there wasn't any will, I knew they'd shoot me.

Britney said, "Let's go! Let's go!" and the Ford shot forward.

Seconds later, Todd swore, and hit the brake.

I sat up.

Two squad cars, blue lights whirling, blocked our path.

"Police!" yelled a voice. "Get out with your hands in the air."

Two officers approached.

"Stay down," Todd told Britney.

She put her head on her knees.

He grabbed the gun and rolled down his window. He was going to shoot the police!

As he raised the gun, I attacked from behind. My hands circled his throat, jerking his head backward. The gun fired into the air.

Todd struggled. I held on. He pointed the gun over his shoulder at me.

Bang! I heard the bullet whiz past my ear and shatter the back window.

Britney looked up, then dug her nails into my arm, trying to pull my hand away.

Bang! This shot came from behind the Ford. One officer had sneaked around and approached from the rear. Todd yelped, and dropped his gun.

Police quickly surrounded us.

"It's your fault!" Britney cried. "We would have been rich!"

An officer read Todd and Britney their rights. They were frisked and handcuffed, and Todd's minor arm wound was treated.

An officer took my name and asked if I was okay.

"Yes. They were going to kill me! You saved my life!"

"And you saved ours," he replied. "Is there an older hostage, too?"

"No. How did you know I was here?"

"We didn't. A police detective followed a tip from a burglary victim and went to question the owner of this property. He found her tied up in her apartment. She said her nephew had kidnapped her sister and was taking her to this address."

"Mrs. Pameron gets confused," I said. "She thought I was Maud."

・・・

My picture was in the paper the next day, under the headline TEEN CATCHES ROBBER, PREVENTS COP SHOOTING. The article said that Todd and Britney had committed twenty burglaries plus the bank robberies. The trunk of his car contained an assault rifle, three laptops, and a bag of cocaine. They sold most of the stolen goods themselves to pawnshops or on eBay and Craigslist, but used Mrs. Pameron as a fence for antiques. They took advantage of her confusion by pretending the goods belonged to Maud. When the reporter contacted Mrs. Pameron's daughter, who lived in another state, she came immediately to help her mother.

That afternoon, Claire came to the shop. "Look," she said, holding out her hand.

"The poison ring!"

"The police found it by the sink in Mrs. Pameron's apartment. Rosie got her computer back, too—all because you spotted my ring and followed that awful woman."

"Which she should not have done," Mom said.

I grinned. After six days of fear, the antiques business was fun again.

DRAGONFLY EYES

· ALANE FERGUSON ·

Monday morning, on the floor of my science classroom, I, Savannah Rose Anderson, woke up dead.

A bullet pierced my skull and my body crumpled beneath me, thudding hard on the school's linoleum floor. There was no pain—no feeling at all but a last quiet breath and then . . . nothing. Now, as I open transparent lids, I realize time and space have bent around me. There is a blankness as I try to comprehend the fact that my soul and body have lost their connection. I have been ripped apart, a cloth rent in two.

"Savannah!" A girl named Claire lunges toward my body as the man who killed me yanks Claire's hair, twist-

ing it around his fist like a scarf until her chin snaps up. With arms strong as cables he shoves the muzzle of the gun into Claire's cheek as he yells at her to shut up. She looks at him with wild eyes. Her heart drums so hard I'm afraid it might burst.

Claire, I whisper.

Somehow I understand that I can move in a way I never did in life. Like steam I rise up toward the ceiling; beneath me I see blood that seeps from my head into a pool of vivid scarlet. My blood. As easily as one snuffs out a candle, I have ceased to be, and yet I still exist. This new state of being confuses me.

One of my shoes has landed three feet away, and my fingers curl from my palm as though they are petals of a flower. It's so strange, truly seeing myself from the outside. Not a reflection of my face in a mirror but the whole of who I was. I know this man shot me but I cannot explain why. I close my eyes and try to remember.

Then my memory returns full force, so that I gasp.

One hour before, I'd been sitting at my desk, listening to Mr. Ward as he explained a dragonfly's prismatic vision while a boy named James yawned sleepily at a desk to my left.

"The dragonfly has amazing sight because as it flies it can scan three hundred and sixty degrees in every direction," Mr. Ward intoned while drawing a hexagon on the whiteboard with a green marker. "A dragonfly has the best perception of any creature on earth. Their senses are almost magical."

And then a loud crack of the door followed by shrill screams as my killer burst inside our classroom, his gun held out in front of him, both hands gripping the handle tight.

"Give me two hostages! I want two! Now, now, now!"

In the end the man had chosen me and Claire. Classmates who could not have been more different—I, who have sparkled all my life, and Claire, quiet, friendless, awkward, strange.

"You with the long blond hair!" he had screamed, pointing directly at me. "And you!" The gun had snapped over to Claire. "I want you both to stand by the window or I'll start shooting your friends! *The rest of you, get out. Move, move, move!*"

In death I see the irony of our lives, mine and Claire's, how they'd become irrevocably intertwined in that one random act. I remember the girls crying, the boys stoic as they shuffle by me in a single file. How Mr. Ward had tried to stay in the room but was forced to leave when my killer shot the window, so that the glass exploded onto the countertop in a galaxy of stars. How Claire and

I had clung to each other while outside police car lights flashed and the fire truck wailed. To my shame I remember this, too—wishing that if one of us should have to die, let it be Claire.

How selfish I was in life. How clear is my vision in death.

"Why did you kill her?" Claire chokes out each word.

"I told them. I *told* them." He releases her hair and kicks the ribs of my body with the toe of his boot. What is left of me rocks gently on the linoleum. "They'll believe me now—I killed the pretty one. She's dead. They'll hear *that*." His breath swirls out of his mouth. I have never seen air before. It's strange, the way I perceive everything, even thoughts, as if I, too, possess the dragonfly's prismatic vision. My killer's name is Drew. Seamed lines fan down to his neck, and there is dirt beneath his fingernails. The soul is twisted and dark as tree roots.

"They only listen to blood!" he shouts. His spittle hits Claire's skin.

Claire is thinking that she has only moments to live and I know she is right. I am swirling above her, powerless. Claire whispers my name so softly that Drew does not hear. I swoop in close so that my forehead almost touches hers. As easily as reading a book I look inside her and I see an amazing thing: Claire's soul is shining. It's filled with some kind of essence, gold and white, bright as the edge of the sun. The girl I had always dismissed amazes me with her light.

With my new sight I follow the threads of her life as they unfurl like ribbons. I follow one and see how she loved James quietly, too shy to speak. There is Claire making dinner in a tiny kitchen, laughing as she drains noodles. I see her looking in a mirror, her mouth pressed into a thin line until she sighs and shakes her head as she walks away. I watch her read a book to a small boy; I see her strain as she cleans garbage from a gutter. There is another strand unwinding. In it I see myself and my friends as we laugh at Claire behind cupped hands. We snicker at her black clothes, her odd hair, whisper at the thickness of her thighs. Claire understood she was an object of our ridicule and yet, amazingly, she grieves that I am gone.

In death I am ashamed.

How can I have been so blind? Nothing on this side matters the way it did when I was alive. Not shoes or the clothes I had so carefully worn. Here there is no status. Love is the only thing that crosses over with the soul, and Claire is filled with it.

"Don't worry, I'll let you live," Drew lies to Claire now. His words are the color of my blood. Panic rises through me and shoots out of my fingers in electric waves. Drew is going to murder Claire and then himself—the pictures flash through his mind. He wants to be remembered forever, a celebrity for eternity. Pages of his manifesto are tucked into the pocket of his jeans.

"No!" I scream. Emotion shoots through me in flames, pulsing through me like a fire to scorch everything inside. My hand hits him, but it passes though him without a mark. I am helpless.

"We're going to the window, you and me," Drew tells Claire. "The police heard that gunshot. They'll want to know which girl is still alive."

He will kill her at the window so that everyone will be a witness. I can taste Claire's fear as she struggles, begging for her life. Her words mean nothing to him.

I concentrate with everything I have, pushing against the molecules of air. Outside, lawmen decide to break into the school, but I know they will be too late. The trigger cocks. Claire squeezes her eyes tight because she feels her own death coming. She pictures her parents and thinks of God.

"Now!" I scream to no one, to everyone.

I don't understand how I do it, but I feel myself compress my spirit into a tiny point and shoot myself into the tip of Drew's trigger finger. Everything inside me pulses as I inhabit his very cells; I feel his blood surge and the adrenaline storm through his veins, but I am matching his energy. I discover I can move his flesh. With that knowledge I strain with everything inside of me.

"What the . . . ?" he cries as the gun inches away from Claire. Cursing, Drew tries to regain control, but I intensify my focus. His eyes go wide as his hand snaps to his own temple. My energy is like a laser as I turn my soul into fire. A shot splits the air. An instant later Drew falls to the floor close to my own broken body as my spirit breaks free. A blackness pools into the floor with a moan and he is gone, a shadow melting.

It is over. The only sound is Claire's ragged breathing.

"Oh my God!" Claire cries, dropping to her knees. Spattered in Drew's blood, she leans over to touch my lifeless body, tears streaming down her face. She cries in loud gulps while I rejoice in the fact that she is alive.

"Savannah," she gasps. "I'm so sorry! I'm so sorry."

The space that separates us seems thin as gauze, but she does not sense that I am still here, right next to her. "It's okay," I tell her. I stroke her head, my hand brushing the coils of her red hair, but she cannot feel me. The energy I had has dissipated and I am once again without touch. I look into my body's blank eyes, a deepwater blue. There is so much I should have done when I was alive, when things mattered. But I was given this one bit of grace. Because of me, Claire will go on.

The police are running inside the building, and I know they are just moments away. When I look ahead I see there will be a huge funeral inside the gym for me, with thousands of flowers emanating their oversweet scent. Everyone will weep and secretly wonder if Claire should have been taken instead of me. The thought makes me sad. Because like a dragonfly, I perceive with a panoramic vision that reveals truth. Neither one of us should have been taken in that wasteful act of violence, but it is Claire, not me, who is destined to accomplish amazing things. The girl I ignored will leave her mark on the world in a way I never could. To know this helps me accept my fate. The understanding is bittersweet, a lesson learned too late on earth, and yet I see a new purpose in my lingering here. From this side I believe the right girl lived.

And I'll be watching her, every day, until we meet again.

JEEPERS PEEPERS

· RYAN BROWN ·

Darkness had fallen, but the late August air still hung hot and thick over the bayou when Elizabeth Nolan finally reached her destination.

The babysitting job had required her to leave her own neighborhood—*where the roads were actually paved!*—and drive halfway around the lake after dark.

Seething at the very idea, she almost turned for home right then, but she knew she couldn't. She needed the money. School started back next week and she had no fall wardrobe to speak of, and a summer spent mostly at the mall or lying by the pool had left her flat broke.

And that's not to mention the good ol' take-some-initiative/show-some-responsibility speech her parents had been giving her.

Resigned, she turned off the ignition. Her ears buzzed with the screech of the crickets and cicadas in the surrounding woods. She opened the driver's door and heard water trickling in the distance. And to her horror, from somewhere much closer by, she heard the wet, throaty croak of a frog.

Great, she thought. *Frogs. How fan-freaking-tastic!*

Steeling herself, she stepped out of the car.

The house was a single-story shack, tucked under sprawling live-oak limbs that wept streams of moss onto its corrugated tin roof. Funny thing about those moss-strewn trees, she thought. Lining the manicured fairways at the country club near her house, they offered a certain majestic beauty. But out here they had a much more depressing effect, adding to the ghostly gloom of the place.

The house was as square as a cracker box, and sat at a tilt on crumbling cinder blocks. It had a screened front door, beyond which a dull light glowed, but Elizabeth couldn't make out anything except yellowing walls inside.

A female figure appeared behind the screen.

"You're late."

Elizabeth stepped onto an elevated porch riddled with rusted tools and bald tires. "Yes. I'm sorry."

The woman didn't open the door, but remained a faceless silhouette behind the screen. "You near enough made *me* late. I can't afford to get m'self fired, you know. Not in my situation." Despite the hostile tone, her words came out slow and cool, almost in a whisper.

Elizabeth swallowed hard. "Again, I apologize. It's sort of a long way out here. And I got a little lost past the fork, where the road veers off into the . . . um . . ."

"*Swamp.*"

"Pardon?"

"Call it what it is. City folk'll call it the bah-yoo, but I say call it what it is."

"Well . . . anyway, I got here as quickly as I could. It *was* a last-minute call, so I had to rearrange my schedule and everyth—"

"I had no choice 'bout that. I's desperate. No one else would come."

Elizabeth didn't even want to think about the meaning of the last comment. "Well, I'm glad I could help out," she said, trying to lighten the exchange. She reached into her purse. "I've got a list of references here if you'd like to see them."

"Would have done. But I don't read too good and

I hadn't the time anyhow. You been sittin' kids long?"

"Since eighth grade. And I used to babysit my cousins sometimes before that."

Elizabeth sensed the woman sizing her up from head to toe, studying her.

"Well," she sighed. "I got no choice. You're here and I gotta be off."

"So where's, uh, Webster?"

"Wilbur."

"Right. Sorry. Wilbur."

"He's gone to bed already. Maybe he won't need no tendin' to at all."

"That's fine. I'm sure I can keep myself busy with—"

"Then again, there's times when my Wilbur needs a little . . ." The woman's words drifted off. She drew a deep breath, then exhaled slowly. "Well, sometimes he needs a little . . . *extra* care. I hope you can see to that."

Her tone had grown eerily sober.

Elizabeth waited a few beats for further explanation that never came. "You mean bad dreams?" she said. "Well . . . sure. I think I can handle that. Is there a number where I can reach you? I could call if I thought there was any reason for concern."

"Ain't no phone here."

"But, when we spoke—"

"I called you from the bait shop up yonder. Mr. Simmons there done me a favor, found your ad on that computer a' his and gave me your number. I's desperate, you see."

"Oh. Okay. Well, it doesn't matter. I brought my cell phone." She dug the phone out of her purse and turned it on. Her stomach sank when the screen came up. "Oh . . . um, unfortunately, I don't seem to be getting a signal."

"You know, I would stay and tend to him m'self if I could," the woman said. "It breaks my heart to hafta leave my boy like this. You believe that, don't you?"

There was a tinge of sadness in her voice now.

Elizabeth stared into the faceless shadow. "Well, yeah. I'm sure if you could—"

"God Almighty, how I hate to leave him. Especially . . . especially in his condition."

The implication made Elizabeth uneasy, but the woman continued before she could ask the nature of the boy's "condition."

"But I got no choice, do I? I got to work to keep him fed and tended to, look after his needs and such. It's just me and him, you see?"

Elizabeth nodded. "Yes. I think I understand. So is there anything . . . *special* I need to know?"

"Anything you need to know, you'll find out, I s'pose."

It wasn't the answer Elizabeth had hoped for. She slapped a mosquito feasting on the back of her neck. The swarming insects were the only thing making her eager to get inside. "I think I can take it from here. You shouldn't be late for work."

"No. I surely shouldn't."

The woman shifted her weight, bringing her face into the glow of the lightbulb dangling from a cord in the room behind her.

Her beauty took Elizabeth aback.

She was younger than Elizabeth had expected given the maturity of her voice, probably mid-twenties. Her skin was flawless and smooth. Her hair was pulled back into a neat bun, stabbed through with a pencil pocked with teeth marks. Her honey-brown eyes looked weary from too much work and too little sleep, and yet, whether she wanted them to or not, the eyes betrayed a palpable kindness. Elizabeth found it strangely disarming and couldn't help but smile.

"What is it?" the woman asked, noticeably defensive.

"Nothing. I just . . ." She didn't know how to answer. Her eyes fell to the charm at the woman's neck—a tarnished *W* hanging from a thin silver chain. "That's pretty," she said, indicating the necklace. "*W* for Wilbur, I'm guessing. Right? He must be very special to you."

The woman seemed flustered by the flattery. "Yes," she said. "He *is* a very special child." The door creaked open and a hand extended across the threshold. "What do they call you again?"

"Elizabeth."

"My name's Grace." They shook. The woman's skin was coarse, but her grip was delicate, feminine. "God bless you for lookin' after my boy." She glanced over her shoulder. "Take good care of him, won't you? He's all I got. I'll be back at dawn."

She moved past Elizabeth and stepped off the porch, trailing a scent of cheap perfume. Turning back, she brought her eyes up slowly. "You seem like a nice girl. I'd have liked to get to know you."

Elizabeth shrugged. "Well, who knows? Perhaps you will."

"No." The woman shook her head and her smile faded. "You won't be back. None of them ever come back a second time."

She turned and started off on foot into the darkness.

The scream came three hours later.

Elizabeth's resting eyes popped open. She shot

upright from the tattered sofa and stood quickly.

Too quickly—she became dizzy. The room was like an oven, stifling and airless. Sweat stung her eyes, forcing them shut again and leaving her completely disoriented.

She felt something brush against the back of her head and spun around in fright, swatting at the air.

Glass shattered.

Broken shards rained down on her.

She opened her eyes again to find herself in total darkness.

It was then that she realized she had just swatted the dangling bulb, sending the house's only light source crashing into the ceiling.

Panic gripped her as another scream rang out of the boy's room, louder than the first.

She ran blindly across the living room and continued past the kitchenette to the closed door at the end of the narrow hall. She fumbled for the knob, then flung open the door.

"Mama!"

Elizabeth rubbed the wall in search of a light switch. "No, Wilbur, it's not your—"

"Help me, Mama! The creepers are comi—"

"Calm down, Wilbur, it was just a bad dream . . ."

"Come, Mama! Please!"

"I'm not your mother, Wilbur!" she called into the darkness. "I'm your babysitter. Everything's okay, now."

"Come! Please!"

Giving up on the search for a light switch, she made a move toward the frightened voice, but tripped on something that sent her tumbling to the floor.

"What happened?" the boy cried.

"It's okay! I just tripped, that's all. Are you all right?"

"I'm s-scared!" he stammered. "I wanna see you! Please, let me touch you!"

She heard his arms slapping the bed.

"I'm coming. Don't be scared." She managed to get to her knees. "Can you reach a lamp, Wilbur, or tell me where one is? I can't see a thing."

"Ain't none."

"You don't have a light in your room?" she exclaimed.

"No, ma'am. No light."

"Well, do you know where your mother keeps the spare bulbs? I seem to have broken the one in the living room."

"Don't know about no bulbs," he said. "She keeps matches in the kitchen, though. Candles, too, I think. I only know 'cause she tole me never to mess with 'em."

"I'm going to step back into the other room and get them."

"No!"

"I'll just be right outside, and I'll keep the door open, okay?"

"Don't leave me!"

"I'm not leaving you, Wilbur. I have to get us some light so we can see."

"Well, then keep talkin'," he pleaded. "Please, miss. Keep on lettin' me hear you when you go."

"I will."

"Promise!"

"I promise."

She made it out of the room and, with her outstretched arms patting madly at the air, she at last found the kitchenette. She could still hear the fright in Wilbur's panting breath and made a point to call out to him every few seconds. After rummaging through cabinets and drawers cluttered with cookware and utensils, her hand fell on what she thought was a candlestick. A quick sniff of vanilla-scented wax confirmed it. She found a box of matches in the same drawer and lit the candle.

When she returned to the bedroom, Wilbur was sitting upright in his bed. His pajamas were soaked with sweat.

Somehow the boy she had pictured in her head didn't look like the boy she saw now. She had imagined a child more . . . well, different—younger perhaps, given the degree of his terror.

He looked to be about eight or nine and had the face of a cherub.

"You okay?" she asked, standing at the door.

"Think so," he whispered. "For now." He wiped the tear streaks from his cheeks.

"It's all over. You woke up, you see. So it's all over now."

"That don't always help, miss . . ."

"Elizabeth."

"Will you come over here, Miss Elizabeth?" His arms reached out toward her.

Taking care about where she stepped this time, she went to him and took a seat on the edge of the bed. The mattress was like a wet sponge. A faded Snoopy sheet lay twisted across it.

"It's okay now." She took his hand and gave it a reassuring squeeze.

He quickly took his hand back.

"Lemme touch *you*." It was the second time he had made the peculiar request. "May I, Miss Elizabeth? Would you mind?"

"Well . . . I . . ."

His hand came up. She winced instinctively as the soft

pads of his fingers began to trace the contours of her face—over her eyes, down both sides of her nose, across her mouth, and under her chin. Then his other hand moved to the top of her head and slowly raked down the length of her hair.

He smiled, a grin missing two lower teeth. "Now I can see you. I reckon you can close your mouth now."

Elizabeth closed her jaw, which had fallen open in shock. "Omigod," she whispered, unable to mask the astonishment in her voice. "You can't see!"

"I'm blind. But I can still see. I know how you look now, that's for sure. You could help me out by tellin' me the color of your hair and eyes, though."

"Um . . . blue."

"You got blue hair?"

"No, I meant . . . I mean I have blue *eyes*. And blond hair."

"I know. I's just teasin' you." A frown creased his face. "Blue eyes? Hmm. Mama says blue is cold. And blond is like yellow, right? A hot color."

"I'm sorry, I don't understand."

"That's how Mama 'splains colors. Says they got a feelin' to 'em. Blue's cold. Yellow's hot. Orange's warm. White don't feel much like nothing at all. And black . . .

well, I got a pretty good idea what black's like. See plenty of that, that's for sure."

His meaning finally dawned on her. "You were born blind. Right? You've never actually seen colors."

"Yep, born blind. Nope, never seen colors. But I can still see. Too good sometimes in fact."

Elizabeth held up the candle and looked around the windowless room. Scattered toys covered the floor. A knife-whittled cross hung from a frayed piece of yarn above the bed. Higher up the wall was what looked like a dotted line of pencil marks, which upon closer inspection was a line of ants moving in single file toward a crack below the ceiling.

There were no posters or picture frames on the scarred walls. She found this odd until it occurred to her that they would make about as much sense as a lamp in the room of a blind child.

He gripped her hand. "Will you stay with me, Miss Elizabeth, beside me, I mean?"

"Yes. Of course."

"All night?"

"Sure. If you want. Are you hungry?"

"No. Thanks."

"Can I get you some fresh pajamas?"

"These're all I got, these here Spider-Mans. They *are* Spidies, aren't they?"

"Sure are. How about if I go and get you a glass of water?"

"No!" His grip became a vise on her arm. "Stay."

"All right, Wilbur. I'll stay."

Satisfied, his grip loosened. His head fell back to the pillow. Elizabeth pulled up the sheet, using a dry corner of it to blot the beaded sweat from his brow.

"It's late," she said. "You better try and get some sleep."

"Please. Can't I stay awake . . . just for a while?"

"Okay. But just a *short* while."

He nodded, and his eyes blinked slowly closed.

Thunder rumbled in the distance. Wilbur's body shuddered at the sound, but Elizabeth's calming hand settled him again.

"Why don't you tell me about your dream," she said.

"What for?"

"Maybe talking about it will make it seem . . . less scary."

Wilbur shook his head. "It's best if I don't. Best if I don't think about it at all. That's the only way to keep 'em away."

"To keep who away?"

"The creepers."

Elizabeth couldn't suppress her smile and hoped that he couldn't sense it. "Who are the creepers?"

"Best to keep 'em right out of my head, Miss Elizabeth. That way they won't come. It's safe when everything stays dark. In my head, I mean."

"What a strange thing to say."

"Why's that?"

"Most people feel just the opposite about the dark. I know when I was a little girl, I was very frightened of it."

"Not me. I feel good when I just see the dark. It's when stuff starts gettin' into my head that things go bad."

"Like when you have a scary dream?"

"Yes, ma'am. Or even when I just get to thinkin' on scary things."

"I was always taught that an active imagination was a good thing, especially for little boys. Wonderful things can come out of it."

"Bad stuff, too," he whispered. "'Specially for someone like me."

"Like you?"

"Blind folks. Mama says folks born blind don't know

the way things really look, just how we imagine 'em. And she says some blind folks even have a *heightened* imagination."

"Sounds like a pretty neat gift to me."

"Yeah. But sometimes mine gets *heightened* too much. Sometimes when I get to thinkin' on things I see in my head, those things just get a little . . . *too* real."

Elizabeth's eyes drifted down to the candle, which had dribbled a puddle of wax at her feet. "Wilbur . . . what do the creepers look like?"

"They changin' all the time. Depends on how I see 'em in my head, or maybe how I dreamed 'em. You understand?"

"No, Wilbur. I'm afraid I don't. Can you explain it to me?"

His eyes opened again. "Please, Miss Elizabeth, don't get me thinkin' 'bout 'em."

"But I think it might help."

"No! Please." He sat up quickly. "I shouldn't be thinkin' on it." Panicked, he pressed his back against the headboard; his heels dug trenches into the mattress.

"Okay, Wilbur. Calm down."

"No." He shut his eyes tightly. "It's already too late!"

She placed a hand on his churning legs in an attempt

to restrain him. "I didn't mean to scare you. Everything's all right."

"No! It's too late, Miss Elizabeth! It don't take 'em long to come once I start seein' 'em. And I can see 'em now! They're already—"

"Wilbur, calm down! This is silly. It's impossible to see things in your head and then suddenly make them come to—"

The explosion of sound from the front room split the air and rocked the entire house.

Elizabeth screamed. The candle slipped from her hand and fell to the floor, plunging the room into darkness.

Wilbur went rigid beside her.

"It's too late," he said in a shaken whisper. "They're here. I'm seein' 'em right now . . . and they're coming for us."

Elizabeth turned to him, her heart a drum in her chest. *It can't be true*, she thought. *It's not possible!*

In the next instant the heavens opened overhead. Rain pelted the tin roof like machine-gun fire.

Lightning flashed, and in the fleeting blue strobe Elizabeth found Wilbur's eyes fixed on the open door.

Thunder crashed again, much closer than before.

Elizabeth leaned toward Wilbur and whispered,

"What's happening, Wilbur? Please, tell me what's happening!"

Before he could answer, another percussive burst of sound shot out of the living room. The house lurched in a crack of splintering wood. Somewhere a window shattered. A warm wind rushed into the room, swirling around them like grabbing hands.

Elizabeth lunged for Wilbur and lifted him off the bed. His arms wrapped tightly around her neck. Clutching him to her chest, she rushed blindly from the room.

She screamed again when she saw what awaited in the front room.

The creepers had already blocked off the only route of escape.

Against the continuous strobes of lightning, they appeared as humanlike shadows, faceless save for a pair of narrow-slit eyes that glowed bright green.

Their movement was lithe, catlike.

Elizabeth saw two of them enter through the open doorway on wiry limbs. The door itself had been ripped from its hinges and now lay in scattered slats across the floor.

Another creeper entered to her left, slithering over the jagged shards of a broken window set high into the wall. Once inside, the creeper proceeded to crawl headfirst down the wall until it reached the floor and came back up in a low, predatory crouch.

A cloud of dust plumed into the room.

Elizabeth turned. Another creeper had come in through the chimney and now stood coiled in a sprinter's pose atop the ashes in the fireplace.

A cannon shot of thunder shook the house.

Wilbur buried his face into Elizabeth's shoulder.

"Make it stop!" he cried. "Please, make it stop! Don't let them get me!"

But the creepers were already circling in. Elizabeth moved backward on trembling legs until she found herself pinned against the wall, her path to the door blocked by the dark figures closing in with slow, calculated steps.

Holding Wilbur close to her chest, she turned her back on them, using her body as a shield.

"Stay away from him!" she shouted. "He's just a little boy!"

Her plea was met with hungry grins—four sets of jagged yellow teeth splitting the width of the creepers' menacing black faces.

They were only five feet away.

Four.

Three.

"They're gonna kill us!" Wilbur cried. "I can see them! Make them go away!"

"I can't!" Elizabeth shook her head desperately. "I don't know what to do!"

No sooner had she said the words than she realized it wasn't she who held the power to save them.

The only one who could rescue them from their stalkers was the one who had created them—the one who had *imagined* them into existence.

Keeping her back to the creepers, she knelt, setting Wilbur's bare feet on the rain-slick floor. It took every ounce of strength she had to pry the boy off of her. Against his protests, she pushed him back far enough to hold his face between her hands.

"Send them away, Miss Elizabeth!" he cried over the howl of the wind. "Please. You gotta send 'em away!"

"I can't do that, Wilbur! Only *you* can!"

"No . . ."

"Wilbur, listen to me! If you can imagine bad things and make them real, then you can do the same with good things. But you have to *choose* to see the good things, Wilbur. You have to imagine them to make it real. It's the only way to beat them, and I can't do it for you!"

The creepers were upon them now.

Elizabeth felt cold, gelatinous fingers on the back of

her neck. She kept her eyes on Wilbur, refusing to move, refusing to let him sense her fear. The hand slithered around to the front of her neck and began to squeeze. Still Elizabeth held firm, unmoving.

The other creepers closed in on Wilbur.

They knelt at the boy's side, their hungry gaze set on his neck, their jaws open wide.

The cold, boneless fingers increased their grip at Elizabeth's throat.

"Come on, Wilbur," she gasped. "You have the power to end this. You can change your fate just by changing your thoughts."

Wilbur's eyes opened as the creepers' gaping jaws went for his neck.

"Stop!" he shouted. *"Stop it right now!"*

The creepers did as ordered.

The glow of their eyes dimmed.

They tilted their heads in confusion, their prey having become their master in an instant.

Elizabeth felt the eel-like fingers loosen at her neck, then fall away.

She struggled to draw breath into her lungs as Wilbur looked at each of the creepers in turn. She realized the boy wasn't just looking *toward* his stalkers, but actually *seeing* them, seeing them as he imagined them.

And when her own eyes moved to the creepers, it became clear that his image of them had changed. He now saw them as he wanted to see them—scared and defeated.

The fear had vanished from his face, replaced by something much bolder, defiant.

"I am not afraid of you," he declared. "And I won't let you do this to me anymore. I created you, and now I will destroy you."

His eyes moved intently toward the ceiling. The swirling wind grew stronger and shifted direction, as though it was being sucked toward the open doorway.

Wilbur's hands reached out and found Elizabeth's shoulders. He squeezed, keeping her close, as the suction of air increased.

The creepers' bodies began to stretch like pieces of warm toffee. They suddenly looked shriveled and weak, their emerald eyes wide with fear. When the force of the wind became too much, they dug their tendril-like fingers into the floor, struggling to hold on.

An infantile cry rang out as the first creeper slid across the floor and flew out into the night as though yanked by a powerful chain. The others followed in quick succession, each clawing futilely at the floor as the wind sucked them out like limp sheets of fabric.

The wind died the instant they were gone.

As though a faucet had been shut off, the rain quickly trickled away. Then a final growl of thunder rolled toward a distant sky.

When silence had fallen over the broken house, Elizabeth reached up and dried the tears from Wilbur's cheeks.

She drew him against her.

They held each other for some time before she led him back to the bedroom, relit the candle, and tucked him into bed.

He took hold of her arm as she stood to go. "I don't want you to leave."

"I'm not leaving."

"But will you come back? Please, you must . . ."

"Of course I'll come back, Wilbur. Did you really have to ask?"

"It's just that they never do."

"They? You mean the ones who came before me? Yes, your mother told me they never come back."

"No. They never do."

She leaned in close to his ear. "Well, I'm coming back, Wilbur. I will always come back. That's a promise."

He smiled, reached up to her face, and once again traced her features with delicate hands.

"If you don't mind my saying so, Miss Elizabeth . . . I think you're beautiful."

"You really think so?"

"I surely do. Beautiful. If only you could see yourself the way I see you . . ."

"Well, thank you, Wilbur. A lady always loves to hear that."

He fell asleep seconds later.

Elizabeth stood and tiptoed out of the room. Shielding the candle flame with her hand, she returned to the living room, crossed to the window, and looked out into the peaceful night.

A cool breeze drifted in through the broken glass.

The candle flickered, and she caught her own reflection in one of the shards—a green face with slick amphibious skin, blotched with spots.

PINEY POWER

· F. PAUL WILSON ·

· ONE ·

Old Man Foster had the signs posted all over his land.

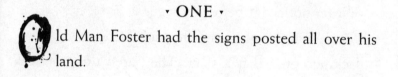

No kidding. And no big deal.

Jack never paid them much attention. He figured since he wasn't involved in the first three, he deserved a pass on the last. No, what caught Jack's eye was the bright red object tacked to the bark just below the sign.

"Hey, check it out," he said, hitting the brakes. His tires skidded in the sandy soil as his BMX came to a stop. "Who'd put a reflector way out here?"

Weezy stopped her bike beside his. "Doesn't make sense."

Her birth certificate said Louise, but no one had called her that since she turned two. She was older than Jack—hit fifteen last week, while Jack still had a few months to go. As usual, she was all in black—sneaks, jeans, Bauhaus T-shirt. She'd wound her dark hair into two braids today, giving her a Wednesday Addams look.

"Never noticed it before."

"Because it wasn't there," she said.

Jack accepted that as fact. They used this firebreak trail a lot when they were cruising the Barrens, and if the reflector had been here before, she'd remember. Weezy never forgot anything. Ever.

He touched the clear sap coating on the head of the nail that fixed it to the tree. His fingertip came away wet. He showed her.

"This is fresh—really fresh."

Weezy touched the goop and nodded. "Like maybe this morning."

Jack checked the ground and saw tire tracks. It had

rained last night, and these tracks weren't washed out in the slightest.

"Looks like a truck," he said, pointing.

Weezy nodded. "Two sets—coming and going. And one's deeper than the other." She looked at Jack. "Hauled something in or took something out."

"Maybe it was Old Man Foster himself."

"Could be."

Foster had supposedly owned this chunk of the Jersey Pine Barrens forever, but no one had ever seen him. No one had ever seen anyone posting the land, either, but the signs were everywhere.

"Want to follow?"

She glanced at her watch and shook her head. "Got to go to Medford with my mom."

"Again? What's this—an every Wednesday thing?"

She looked away. "No. Just works out that way." When she looked back, disappointment shone in her eyes. "You going without me?"

Jack sensed she wanted them to go together, but he didn't think he could hold off.

"Yeah. Probably nothing to see. If I find anything, we can come back together."

She nodded and offered half a smile. "Sure you won't get lost without me?"

He glanced at the sun sliding down the western sky. Every year, people—mostly hunters—entered the Barrens and were never seen again. Folks assumed they got lost and starved. No big surprise in a million-plus acres of mostly uninhabited pine forest. If a vanilla sky moved in, you could lose all sense of direction and wander in circles for days. But with the sun visible, Jack knew all he had to do was keep heading west and he'd hit civilization.

"I'll manage somehow. See you later."

He watched her turn her Schwinn, straddle the banana seat, and ride off with a wave. After the trees had swallowed her, Jack turned off the fire trail and began following the tire tracks along the narrow passage—little more than two ruts separated by a grassy ridge and flanked by the forty-foot scrub pines that dominated the Barrens. They formed a thick wall, crowding the edges of the path, reaching over him with their crooked, scraggly branches.

The passage forked and the tracks bore to the right. A half-dozen feet into the fork he spotted another reflector. At the next fork the tracks bore left, and sure enough, another reflector.

Odd. He'd figured the first had been a marker for the starting point of the trail. Grass and trees could thicken over a growing season and obscure what had once been an obvious opening. But whoever had come along here this morning was marking every turn, placing reflectors where headlights would pick them up as they approached. That meant he was planning to come back in the dark. Maybe tonight. Maybe many nights.

Why?

Jack found the answer a half mile farther on where the tire tracks ended in a clearing with a large, solitary oak in its center. Near its base someone had dumped a dozen or more fifty-five gallon oil drums—old ones, rusted, banged up, and leaky.

He jumped at the sound of a car engine roaring his way. A few seconds later a weird-looking contraption bounced into the clearing on the far side. It had the frame of a small Jeep, maybe a Wrangler, with no roof, sides, or hood. The engine was exposed, though the fire wall was still in place, and instead of a steering wheel, someone had fixed a long-handled wrench to the column. The front and rear seats had been replaced by a pair of ratty-looking sofas occupied by three kids in their mid-teens. Jack recognized the driver: Elvin Neolin from his civics class. He'd seen the other boy around school as well, but the white-haired girl was new.

Pineys.

They lived out here in the woods. Some had jobs in the towns around the Pines, and some lived off the land—hunting, fishing, gardening. All were poor and a few were a little scary-looking in their mismatched, ill-fitting clothes and odd features. Hard to say why they seemed odd. Not like they had bug eyes and snaggle-teeth; more like looking at a reflection in one of those old-time mirrors where the glass wasn't even.

Some folks called them inbreds, talking about brothers and sisters getting together and having kids. Jack didn't know if any of that was true. People liked to talk, and some people just naturally exaggerated as they went along. But no one could deny that some Pineys didn't look quite right.

The kid riding shotgun was Levi Coffin, a sophomore at SRB High. Coffin was an old Quaker name that Jack envied. Jack Coffin . . . how cool to have a name like that.

Levi jumped out and strode toward Jack. He was tall and lanky, and his clothes were too short in the arms and legs. His mismatched eyes—one blue and one brown—blazed.

"This your doin'?"

Jack tensed. Levi looked a little scary.

"No way. I just got here." He jerked a thumb over his

shoulder, north. "Followed tire tracks from back there. They ended here."

Levi glanced over his shoulder at Elvin, who was staring his way. Elvin was on the short side with piercing dark eyes, stiff black hair, and high cheekbones. Looked like he might have some Lenape Indian in him.

Their eyes locked, then Levi turned away, muttering, "All right, all right."

What's that all about? Jack wondered.

Levi inspected the tire tracks while Elvin hopped out and walked over to the drums. Jack sensed the white-haired girl staring at him from the buggy. He realized with a start that she had pink irises. White hair . . . milk-white skin . . . what was that called . . . ?

Albino . . . she was an albino.

"I can't see him, Levi," she said in a high-pitched voice.

Was she blind?

"What?" Levi swiveled to stare at Jack.

Elvin was struggling with the top to one of the drums. He looked toward Levi, who turned back, then gave his head a sideways jerk toward Jack.

Elvin nodded, saying, "Hey, Levi. Gimme a hand."

Levi walked over and touched the lid—barely touched it—and it popped loose.

Jack felt a funny sensation ripple down his spine as he

remembered an incident in school with Levi. Something way strange here. He hesitated, then started toward the drums as the two boys lifted the lid. They dropped it when they saw what was inside.

"Damn!" Levi said. "Damn them to hell!"

Jack might have quipped about where else you could damn someone to, but the rage in Levi's voice warned him off. He stepped up and saw the thick, cloudy green liquid; his nose stung from the sharp chemical odor.

"What is it?"

"Some sort of toxic crap," Levi said. "They're using this spot as a dumping ground."

"Who?"

"Crooks from upstate. We've found stuff like this before."

Jack said, "Better than dumping it in some river, I guess."

Levi glared at him and pointed to a barrel on its side. The sand near its top was wet with gunk.

"That one's leaking. It sinks into the groundwater. And guess who gets their water from wells out here. *We* do. But who cares about Pineys."

Jack understood some of the reaction. Kids at school tended to rag on the Pineys, make fun of their clothes, joke about the brother-sister connections. But Jack wasn't one of those and didn't like being lumped in with them.

"No fair."

Another look passed between Levi and Elvin, and then Levi shrugged. "Forget it. El says you're okay."

Fine, but Jack hadn't heard El say anything.

"We should tell the cops," Jack said. "My sister used to date a deputy and—"

Levi and Elvin and the girl were shaking their heads . . . same direction, same speed, moving as one. Jack was getting creeped.

"Uh-uh," Levi said. "Cops ain't gonna go patrolling the Pines looking for someone they don't know, who might or might not come back."

"Oh, they'll be back."

Levi's eyes narrowed. "How do you know?"

"Because they marked the path with reflectors."

"Yeah? Show us."

As Jack reached for his bike, Elvin pointed to the weird buggy. "With us."

"You're old enough to drive?"

The two boys laughed.

"Plenty old enough to drive," Levi said. Elvin never said much at school and didn't seem to have much more to say out here. "Just not old enough for a license."

"Aren't you af—?" Jack began, then cut himself off.

of being caught? Out here? By what—the Jersey
n a sheriff's Stetson? Stupid question.

spotted a *Piney Power* sticker on the rusted rear
bumper.

"What's that mean?"

Levi shrugged. "Some folks hereabouts think Pineys
should get organized and vote and all that." He glanced
at Elvin. "We just like the sound of it."

Elvin laughed. "Yeah. Sounds cool."

The girl said nothing, simply stared at him.

Jack gave the buggy another once-over. Without sides,
a top, or even a roll bar, it had to be the most dangerous
car he'd ever seen. He'd be risking his life in that thing.

"Well," Levi said, "you ridin' or not?"

Jack couldn't wait.

"Wouldn't miss it for the world."

As he seated himself on the rear sofa, the albino girl
scooched away and squeezed against the far end. Her
pink gaze never wavered from his face.

"I can't see him."

"Yeah?" Levi turned in the front sofa and looked at
Jack. "El says he's okay."

"But I can't *see* him!"

Jack waved his hand between them and she flinched.

"You can see me."

"That's Saree," Levi said. "She's talking about a different kind of seeing."

Jack was going to ask what he meant but then Elvin started the engine with a roar.

Trying to ignore Saree's unwavering stare, he directed El down the path, following his own bike tracks, till they came to the firebreak trail. El turned around and drove back.

Levi was right. The Burlington County Sheriff's Department didn't have the manpower to stake out Old Man Foster's land or even this one path. Could be weeks before the dumpers made a return trip. Had to be a way to make them give themselves away. Or better yet . . .

An idea began to form.

"What's down that way?" Jack said, pointing left as they approached the first fork.

"More of the same," Levi said. "Why?"

"Wondering if there's a Spong nearby . . . the deeper and wetter the better."

"I know a cripple," Saree said, still staring.

El followed her directions through a few more forks that left Jack totally disoriented.

"You know where we are, right?"

Saree rolled her eyes.

Okay, dumb question to ask a Piney. But at least she seemed to be relaxing a little.

A few minutes later, she said, "Right up here."

El rolled to a stop before a thirty-foot-wide cripple—a water-filled depression half surrounded by white cedars. Without the cedars it would have been called a Spong.

Jack couldn't help smiling when he saw it.

"Yeah, this'll do."

"Do what?"

When he told them their eyes lit. Saree even smiled.

"I still can't see you," she said. "But I think you're okay."

Weird. Too weird.

· TWO ·

What's wrong with inbreeding?" Jack said as he spooned some niblets into the well he'd made in his mashed potatoes.

His mother gasped. "Not at the dinner table."

"No, really. I want to know."

His father cleared his throat and adjusted his steel-rimmed glasses. "Thinking of marrying Kate?"

Kate laughed as Jack said, "No!"

His folks sat at opposite ends while Jack and his older

sister, Kate, sat across from each other. Only his missing brother, Tom, kept it from being a full family meal. Jack didn't miss him. Tom was a pain.

"Then where's this coming from?"

Jack shrugged. "Kids at school talk about Pineys . . ."

He couldn't get those weird kids out of his mind. They seemed so different . . . like they had their own language . . . an unspoken one. And that lid on the barrel . . . Elvin couldn't budge it, but Levi just touched it and it popped free. It reminded Jack of the time Levi and Jake Shuett faced off in the caf a couple of weeks ago over some remark Jake had made about Pineys. Suddenly a ketchup pack Jake was holding squirted all over him and his lunch plate dumped in his lap. Jack had written it off to a spaz attack. He hadn't given it much thought, but now . . .

He wasn't expecting much information from his folks, but Kate was home on a laundry run from medical school—it was only in Stratford, barely thirty miles away—and maybe she'd know.

He glanced at her. "Why's it bad?"

Kate was slim with pale blue eyes and faint freckles. After starting med school she'd cut her long blond hair back to a short, almost boyish length. Jack still wasn't used to it.

She paused, then said, "It's bad because we all have defective 'recessive genes' hidden in our DNA that are passed on from parent to child. Now, as long as that defective recessive gene is matched up with a working gene, all is well. But if a mother and a father both have the same recessive gene, and each gives it to a child, that child could have problems."

"I saw an albino girl today—"

She nodded. "Perfect example: Two normal-skinned parents, each carrying an albino gene, have a one-in-four chance of having an albino child. Family members tend to share a lot of the same recessives, and so inbreeding— when close relatives have children—increases the risk of genetic diseases, because the closer you're related, the greater the odds of matching up the same recessives in your kids."

Now the important question: "But are all recessive genes bad? Could there be ones for, like, big muscles or a good memory?"

Kate smiled. "You're thinking. That's good. Yes, plants and animals are bred for drought resistance and giving more milk and the like."

"Well, in that case, inbreeding people could have some good effects, right?"

"Theoretically, yes. But for every Einstein or Muhammad Ali, you could get a number of kids with cystic fibrosis."

Or weird powers?

Or maybe I read too much science fiction, Jack thought.

· THREE ·

He awoke to the sound of someone whispering his name . . . coming from the window. He hopped out of bed and crossed his darkened room. The high moon lit the grinning face on the far side of the screen.

"Levi?"

"Would you believe they came back again tonight?"

Jack felt his heart rate kick into high gear. "They took the bait?"

"Hook, line, and sinkhole. Figured since it was your idea, you oughta come see. We got the car. Wanna?"

"Be right there."

He pulled on jeans and a rugby shirt, stepped into his Vans, then unlatched the screen and slipped into the night. Levi led him around the corner to where Elvin and Saree were waiting in the buggy, Saree behind the wheel—no, wrench. Her white hair looked silver in the moonlight. They hopped in and Saree took off without a word. At least she couldn't stare at him.

The Pines were practically in Jack's backyard, but she entered along a path he didn't know. She made seemingly random turns through the trees but appeared to know where she was going. Finally she stopped in a small clearing.

"Gotta walk from here," Levi said, "else they'll hear us."

The four of them hopped out, and this time Saree led the way, single file, down a deer path.

"They fell for it, Jack," Levi said from behind him. "Just like you said. I never would've thought of that in a million years. You got a twisted mind. I like that."

Jack enjoyed the praise, but thought the solution had been obvious. Whoever had dumped those barrels didn't know the Pines, otherwise they wouldn't have needed to post reflectors. So Jack's idea had been to move the reflectors off the path to the dumping ground and onto a path that led to the cripple instead.

He heard angry voices before he saw anyone. Saree slowed her pace and gradually a glow began to grow through the trunks. They crouched as they neared the tree line. Jack peeked through the underbrush and saw a flatbed truck angled nose down into the cripple. Its headlights were still on and its motor running. A blue tarp covered whatever was stacked in its bed. Its front end sat bumper-deep in the water, and its rear wheels had dug ruts in the soil from trying to reverse its way out.

One man was cursing and swearing as he stood in the two-foot-deep water and pushed against the front grille while another gunned the engine and spun the tires.

"Now that we've got them," Jack said, "what do we do with them? Call the sheriff?"

Levi shook his head. "No way. We bring in some grown-ups. They'll take care of them."

"Take care of them how?"

"Piney justice."

Piney justice . . . Jack had heard about that. He was going to say something, but right then the one in the water gave up pushing and slammed a hand on the hood.

"Ain't gonna happen, Tony!"

Tony—dark, heavyset with a thick mustache—jumped out and began kicking the water in a rage.

"Save it, man," said the other guy as he splashed past him, heading toward the rim of the cripple. "We're gonna have to off-load this stuff to get outta here."

"How'd this happen, Sammy? We marked the trail!"

"Must've made a wrong turn. Or . . ." He stopped and looked around. "Or somebody moved the markers."

Tony stared at him. "Who?"

"Wiseass locals, my guess. Probably out there right now having a good laugh."

Uh-oh, Jack thought. Time to leave.

"Yeah?" Tony reached into the truck cab and pulled out a revolver. "Well, laugh at this!"

He began firing wildly. One of the slugs zipped through the brush between Jack and Saree, narrowly missing them. Jack froze in terrified shock while Saree let out a shrill yelp of surprise.

"There!" Sammy shouted, pointing their way.

Levi yanked on Jack's arm. "Run!"

Jack didn't need to be told twice—or even once. The next half minute became a riot of crouched running, snapping brush and branches, darkness ahead, shouting behind, and then a high-pitched scream that brought everything to an abrupt, panting halt.

"Saree?" Levi said, looking back. "I thought she was— aw, man, they got Saree!" He turned to Jack. "Go with El for help!"

"You're staying?"

He nodded. "Can't leave her."

Jack wavered. Why had he come here? He wanted to be home. Then Saree screamed again.

"I'll stay with you."

"No way. You go—"

"El doesn't need help. Saree does."

El was already at the car, starting it up. He wasn't waiting. That settled it.

"I don't get it," Levi said as he turned and started back toward the cripple.

"What's there to get?"

"You don't owe her. She's not kin."

Jack couldn't see what that had to do with anything. He wished he'd stayed in bed, but he was here now.

"We came together, we leave together."

Levi didn't reply. They were almost back to the cripple.

"Come out, come out wherever you are," a voice was singsonging. "We got your ugly girlfriend."

Jack peeked through the brush. The moonlight and backwash from the headlights revealed Tony standing on the rim of the cripple by the rear of the truck. He had his gun in one hand and a fistful of Saree's hair in the other. She looked terrified.

Sammy, standing a few feet to his right, shouted, "The rest of you get out here now. We ain't gonna hurt you. Just put you to work. You got us into this mess, so you're gonna get us out."

Jack saw three options. Help was on the way, so until it arrived they either could do nothing, find ways to distract them, or show themselves and do whatever they wanted.

"Get out here or this could get ugly," Tony said, twisting Saree's hair and making her wince. "You don't wanna see *how* ugly."

Jack winced, too, and crossed doing nothing off the list. He decided on distraction. He could always show himself if that didn't work.

"Stay here," he whispered. "Gonna try something."

"Wait—" Levi grabbed for his arm but Jack pulled out of reach.

He moved counterclockwise along the tree line, feeling around the ground until he found a fist-size hunk of shale.

Perfect.

He backed up, cocked his arm, and let fly toward the truck. The rock bounced off the tarp with a gonging sound, then splashed in the water.

"Son of a bitch!" Sammy yelled, flinching.

"You guys deaf?" Tony shouted. "Remember what I said about things getting ugly?"

Oh no. Jack's gut knotted as he saw Tony yank Saree backward. She lost her balance and fell into the water.

Tony stayed with her and held her head under the surface as her arms and legs thrashed and splashed. It was only a couple of feet deep, but plenty enough to drown her.

"She stays under till you come out!" Tony yelled.

Jack couldn't take it. Only option three remained.

"Okay! Okay!"

His bladder ached to empty as he jumped out of the bushes with his hands raised.

To his left Levi also stepped out, hands high, saying, "Let her up!"

As Sammy started toward them, Tony pointed the gun their way and grinned. "When I'm damn good and ready. You kids—*aah!*" He dropped the gun and released Saree as he grabbed his right hand with his left. "She broke my finger!"

Saree sat up, choking and gasping and crying. Jack had seen one of her thrashing arms come near Tony's hand, but no way it touched him. She lurched to her feet and staggered away toward dry ground.

Tony started after her. "You little—my gun!" He turned and bent, feeling around underwater.

As Sammy turned to look at his buddy, Jack took off toward Saree. He grabbed her outreached hand and pulled her up the bank of the cripple.

Sammy started toward them. "Hey—!"

Suddenly he tripped and fell face-first into the water. But instead of rebounding to his feet, he stayed down and began kicking and thrashing as Saree had. He couldn't seem to get up.

Tony finally noticed. "What the hell are you doing?"

He started toward Sammy but tripped himself. He went down and stayed down, too. Were they stuck in the mud? No, their arms and legs were free. It almost looked like they were being held down. But—

Jack saw Levi on his knees, white-faced, eyes focused on the men in the cripple. As Jack headed for him, Saree grabbed his arm.

"Leave Levi be."

Jack pulled free. As he neared he could see the boy's lips pulled back in a snarl. His face and hair dripped sweat, his shirt was soaked, and air hissed between his clenched teeth like he was bench-pressing twice his own weight.

"Levi . . .?"

He glanced at Jack and just then the two men in the cripple got their heads back above water. But not for long. Before they could draw a full breath, they plunged their faces back beneath the surface.

And then everything seemed to happen at once. Elvin

roared out of the trees in the buggy followed by a pick-up full of rough-clothed men with shotguns. Levi let out a breath and slumped forward onto his hands; the two men in the cripple got their heads out of water and sucked air.

When they caught their breath and looked around, they found themselves staring into the headlights of the buggy and the pickup, and down the muzzles of half a dozen shotguns. One of the Piney men, tall with a gray beard and features that looked like they'd been taken apart and put back together wrong, had lifted the tarp and was looking at the barrels hidden beneath.

"Not good," he said, shaking his head. "Not good ay-tall."

"You don't wanna mess with us," Tony said, still panting. "We're connected, if you know what I mean."

"I'm right sure of that," the old Piney said. "And we'll want to know who to." He swiveled and his gaze fell on Jack. "Who's this 'un?"

"Friend of ours," Levi said, rising to his feet. He'd caught his breath. "He set the trap."

"Well, we're right grateful for that, but he ain't one of us. Take him back wherever he came from."

"What about them?" Jack said, pointing to Tony and Sammy.

"You forget about them. We're all gonna have us a nice chat, then we'll send 'em home."

"But—"

Levi grabbed his arm and pulled him away. "No questions. Let's go."

El and Saree were already in the buggy. As soon as Jack and Levi settled on the rear couch, El put it in gear and they roared off.

"What happened back there?" Jack said.

He was feeling weak and shaky. That guy had almost drowned Saree, and he'd never been shot at before—never dreamed it would ever happen and never wanted it to happen again. Ever.

Levi shook his head. "Nothing. And don't go yakking about it."

"You kidding? Tell my folks I snuck out tonight to see some toxic dumpers we trapped and wound up getting shot at? Yeah, right. Soon as I get home I'm gonna run into their bedroom and blab all about it."

Levi laughed. "Okay."

Of course he'd tell Weezy. She'd eat it up.

But he hadn't been talking about the dumpers.

"I meant you. What did you do to those guys?"

The smiled vanished. "Nothing."

"But I saw—"

Levi stared straight ahead. "You saw a couple of guys slipping around on a mucky cripple bottom and getting stuck. That's all."

Jack was sure it had been more than that. But what exactly?

Saree turned to face him. "Yeah, that's all it was, Jack. But what about you? What's your talent? Is it being able to hide? Is that why I can't see you?"

What was she talking about?

"I don't have any talent."

"Maybe you just don't know about it yet. You're hiding something, but that's okay. You came back for me. I never expected that. I still can't see you, but I like you."

Jack had no idea how to respond to that, so he didn't.

They dropped him off about a block from his house. As they raced off he saw their bumper sticker flash in the moonlight.

PINEY POWER.

He had an idea why those kids liked the sound of it.

· FOUR ·

can't believe all that happened without me," Weezy said as they entered Jack's house through the kitchen.

He'd waited till after school to tell her about it.

"Believe me, you were better off at home." He shuddered at a vision of that Tony guy holding Weezy's head underwater instead of Saree's. "While it was happening, I wanted to be anywhere but there."

As they stepped into the front room where his folks were watching the six-thirty news, a TV reporter said, *"The two bodies found inside those barrels of toxic waste have been identified."*

Jack stiffened as he recognized the mug shots on the screen.

"Anthony Lapomarda and Santo 'Sammy' Carlopoli have long rap sheets. Their bodies were found outside a South Philly body shop this morning along with two dozen barrels of toxic waste. More waste was found inside the body shop, along with a number of stolen cars. The suspected chop shop—"

He nudged Weezy and whispered, "That's them!"

The old Piney's parting words came back: *We're all gonna have us a nice chat, then we'll send 'em home.*

He hadn't mentioned *how* they'd be sent home. Jack glanced at Weezy and found her staring back with wide, dark eyes.

"Piney justice," he said, feeling a chill.

His father looked up. "What?"

"Nothing."

Dad pointed to the TV. "That's why we live out here. To get away from scum like that. You don't have to worry about running into any of their sort in these parts."

"I guess not, Dad."

At least not anymore.

THE NIGHT HUNTER

· MEG CABOT ·

verton's was the only place that was hiring the day Nina found out her mother had lost her college fund. But, if she wanted anything more than a secondary education, she had to go looking for a part-time job.

So Overton's it was, even though ordinarily, Nina wouldn't have been caught dead in a preppy store like that.

Which is why Nina was stuck working at the mall that Friday night with Angela Overton. Who was, as usual, trying to get Nina to tell her where all the major parties were that weekend.

"I heard Lauren van der Waals's parents are going to

Boston for the weekend," Angie was saying as she hogged the only stool behind the register. "Misty Johnson and Feather Haynes were talking about it in the ladies'."

There'd been a big sale at Overton's, and Nina was tired from the rush of customers. Her feet hurt. She wouldn't have minded a turn on the stool.

But Angela's parents owned Overton's, and if Nina didn't want Angela to complain to her mother about her, there wasn't much she could say in protest. She didn't think Mrs. Overton would fire her—Nina was one of Overton's best employees—but Mrs. Overton might reassign one of her valuable weekend shifts. Nina couldn't afford to lose either of those. Saturday and Sunday were the only eight-hour shifts she could take, because of school.

Nina told herself she didn't care too much about not getting to sit down. She'd kept her mind off her sore feet by calling the mall radio station approximately every fifteen minutes and asking them to play her favorite song, "The Night Hunter." Jerry, who was on duty at the sound desk, kept saying, "No problem."

But he never played it. Nina hadn't really expected him to, since "The Night Hunter" wasn't exactly the kind of song the Calder Mall played over its sound system. Still, it was a local favorite. Everyone in Eastport loved hearing stories about the Night Hunter—whether they were true or not (. . . and Nina suspected the Eastport Police Department wished they weren't)—Everyone was just as wild as she was about the song local band Witch Hunt had written about him.

Nina's calling Jerry every quarter of an hour also served as a way to interrupt Angela as she droned on about Lauren van der Waals's party.

"Huh," Nina said now, in response to Angela.

"You and Lauren are tight, right, Nina?" Angela asked. "You must be going to her party. It's tomorrow night. I heard Ryan Calder might be going. You know him, right? Or you've at least heard of him. Everybody's heard of him. He's so rich . . . and *hot*. And I heard Lauren say he'd be dropping by. I've just got to meet him. . . ."

"Uh-huh," Nina said. Sometimes she said "uh-huh" to Angie, instead of "huh," to vary her responses. The only reason she bothered responding at all was that Angela's mother was Nina's boss. Nina thought Angela was spoiled beyond belief. Look at the thing with the stool. Angela hadn't once offered to let Nina sit on it. In four hours. "Hang on a minute."

Nina picked up the phone and dialed the number for the Calder Mall radio station. When Jerry at the desk picked up, she said, "Hey, it's Nina at Overton's again.

When are you guys going to play 'The Night Hunter' by Witch Hunt?"

"It's next up on the rotation," Jerry lied. They both knew it was a lie, but Nina said, "Oh, great, thanks, Jerry," and hung up.

"I mean, it's not that I want to meet him for his money or anything," Angela went on. "I know his family built this mall and, well, everything in Eastport, practically. It's just . . . he's so cute! Those blue eyes! And I feel so sorry for him, with his parents getting killed last year. I know I could make him feel better."

I bet you think you could, Nina thought. *And it has way more to do with his bank account than those blue eyes of his.*

Not that Nina knew Ryan Calder that well, either. She'd seen him at a few parties, but had felt weird about approaching him because he'd always been surrounded by girls just like Angie, trying to get into his . . . wallet.

But she knew she'd recognize those piercing eyes of his anywhere—especially since she'd seen them so many times, staring up at her from the pages of the *Eastport News*. There were always photos of him showing up, cutting the ribbon to a new hospital wing paid for by the foundation he'd started in his parents' memory.

"Look," Angie was saying. "I could give you a lift tomorrow night. To Lauren's. If you want."

"Can't," Nina said. "I'm working here tomorrow night."

"I know," Angie said. "I meant after work. I'll pick you up and take you to the party."

"I don't know, Ange," Nina said idly, leaning on the counter and gazing out of the store, across the atrium, where the mall's waterfall cascaded down from the second floor in front of the glass elevators. Mothers with young children, tired of pushing strollers, often sat there to rest, giving their toddlers pennies to throw into the pool. Across the pool, Eastport Bank was beginning to shut down for the night. Nina watched as the tellers put their CLOSED signs up at their booths. "Your mom's got me on the schedule to do inventory all day. I don't know if I'll feel much like going to a party. I'll probably be pretty tired." Nina didn't know why she was giving Angela such a hard time.

Maybe it was because Angela hadn't given her a turn on the stool all night.

"Please?" Angela looked desperate. "Look, I'm not invited to Lauren's party. You are. If you go with me tomorrow night, I'll give you a ride home tonight, too. Then you won't have to take the bus home. You know how unsafe it is, waiting all alone at that bus stop here, after all the stores close and everyone goes home."

Nina did know. That's why she'd been thinking that

what she needed was a boyfriend. A boyfriend with a car, who could pick her up after work. It was no use saving up to buy her own car. Thanks to her mom, she needed to save every penny for tuition in the fall.

But a boyfriend . . . that was doable. As she watched Rick, the security guard, begin to pull down the gates in front of the bank, she went over in her head the various boys she knew. Were any of them really boyfriend material? Not so much . . . Nina had her schoolwork to worry about, after all, and this job. She didn't have time to cater to the whims of some guy. Especially some spoiled rich guy like Ryan Calder.

Unless, of course, she ended up with a guy like . . . well, the Night Hunter.

But of course, that was ridiculous. The Night Hunter didn't have a girlfriend. How did the song go? *He rides alone/Just a rolling stone. . . .*

Yeah, and rolling stones didn't hang out with high school girls. Even seniors who were only a few credits away from graduating.

But if he'd really saved all those people from those violent criminals, just by showing up at the right time and looking intimidating . . .

"Just say you'll come with me," Angela said, breaking

in on Nina's thoughts. "I'll get to the party, and you'll get home safe. I'll feel a lot less guilty about leaving you waiting at that dark bus stop."

Nina thought that if Angela were really as nice as she pretended to be, she'd just give her a ride home without making her promise to escort her to Lauren's party first. Nina's house was actually on the way to Angela's, so it wasn't like it would be any trouble.

But she supposed this was how rich people got that way—never giving away anything for free. The Overtons were among the richest families in Eastport—rumored to be second wealthiest only to Ryan Calder, sole heir to the Calder family fortune now that his parents had been killed in that horrible burglary-gone-awry last year. Yet Nina had noticed Angela was almost always first in line whenever any other store in the mall was having a free giveaway of anything.

"Uh, that's okay," Nina said, lifting up the phone to call the Calder Mall radio station again, and so end her conversation with Angela. "I'll grab a ride with Katie from the bank, or someone."

What did she want to go to a stupid party at Lauren's for, anyway? None of those people wanted to hang out with her anymore, now that she was broke. It was better for Angela to learn now that Lauren and those guys—the Ryan Calders of the world—would only be your friend when you were on top of the world. As soon as you hit bottom, like Nina had, thanks to her mom, it was *See ya, wouldn't wanna be ya.*

It was as she was waiting for Jerry to pick up that Nina noticed something curious happening across the atrium. A tall man in a long black trench coat had come striding down the concourse, heading with decided purpose toward the bank, the gates of which Rick hadn't fully pulled down. Something was wrong with his face. At first Nina couldn't figure out what it was.

Then, a second later, she figured it out. He was wearing a mask. A terrible, grinning clown mask. It was as she realized this that the tall man ducked beneath the half-lowered gate in front of the Eastport Bank. When Rick, the security guard, stepped forward to say something to him, the man pulled something long and skinny from the depths of the black leather trench coat and pointed it at him.

That's when Rick put his hands in the air.

"Oh," Nina cried, a physical shock seeming to jolt through her, not unlike the time she accidentally stuck her finger in the electrical socket while plugging in the toaster. "Oh, my God."

"This is Jerry," Jerry said, answering the phone she still held to her ear.

"Oh, my God, Jerry," Nina said, into the phone. "He's robbing the bank. He—someone's robbing the mall branch of Eastport Bank."

"Who is this?" Jerry asked. "Nina? Is that you?"

"It's me," Nina said. Her lips felt numb. She watched as the man with the gun made Rick lie down on the bank floor. "Call nine-one-one. Someone's robbing the bank."

"Are you kidding me?" Jerry wanted to know. "Is this a joke because I wouldn't play that Night Hunter song?"

"No, it's not a joke," Nina cried, even as Angela, who'd seen what was going on, had dived behind the counter, and was tugging on Nina's arm to do the same. "It's happening right now. There's a man in a clown mask wearing a black leather trench coat robbing the bank. He has a gun. Call nine-one-one right now! Oh, never mind, I'll do it—"

Slamming the phone down into its cradle, Nina picked it back up and dialed, then handed the phone to Angela, crouched behind the register.

"Wh-what are you doing?" Angela demanded, staring at the phone as if it were a snake about to bite her.

"I'm going out there to see what I can do to help," Nina said. "Tell nine-one-one what's going on."

"Are you *insane?*" Angela demanded as Nina slipped out from behind the counter. "It's him! It's the Night Hunter!"

"No, it isn't," Nina said, instantly incensed. "The Night Hunter *helps* people. He doesn't rob them."

"But they say he wears a mask! And that guy—"

"Night Hunter wears a mask so he won't be recognized and punished for being a vigilante," Nina snapped. Of all the people she could have been forced to work with, why did it have to be Angela Overton, the stupidest girl on the planet? "And it's a black mask, not a *clown* mask. Now stay here."

"Wh-where are you going?" Angela whispered. "What are you going to do? You can't do anything to help those people! *You're* not the Night Hunter!"

Nina wished she were. She wished she were the Night Hunter. She'd stop the man holding up the bank. She'd force her mother to get her college money back from the boyfriend she'd given it to. She'd also have a cool motorcycle to ride around on. The first thing she'd do as the Night Hunter would be to quit working at Overton's.

"I'm not the Night Hunter," she said. "But I can try to make sure that man doesn't hurt anyone." The Night Hunter did it. Why couldn't she? Her heart was pounding in her chest. How she was going to do this, she had no idea. "Just talk to the operator. Have they picked up?"

"You're crazy," Angela said, shaking her head, her eyes glittering. "Just stay here. You can't leave me alone! I . . . I'll tell my mother!"

Through the phone, Nina could hear a voice asking, "Ma'am? Are you there? Ma'am, this is nine-one-one, how can I help you?"

"Tell them what's going on," Nina said, nodding to the phone Angela still clutched in her hands. "I have to go see what I can do to help. You'll be all right here. Just tell the police to hurry."

"Don't leave me!" Angela wailed.

But Nina was already walking out of the store and heading around the waterfall and pool toward the bank. It was odd listening to the music playing over the mall's sound system—the light rock Jerry always played when it was late. He'd only put on the good stuff now, when the stores had begun closing, and customers were starting to head home—tonight, while watching a man in a trench coat and clown mask forcing the bank tellers to come out from their booths.

That's Katie, Nina thought as she saw the man in the mask grab one teller who hadn't moved quickly enough and push her roughly to the floor. Katie just had a baby last spring.

Shoppers were coming toward her end of the mall. And they had kids. Nina knew she had to do something. She had to do something to warn people away from this end of the mall. That's what the Night Hunter would do. He'd try to help. Why hadn't Jerry—stupid Jerry—made an announcement over the sound system? Had he even bothered calling the police?

Then, as she glanced around in desperation, she saw it. Of course. The fire alarm on the wall by the courtesy telephone. This wasn't a fire. But the system would go off mall-wide, and shoppers would know to evacuate. She'd stay put and warn them not to use this exit. . . .

Nina ran for the alarm and pulled it. A split second later, the alarm was sounding in earsplitting whoops, accompanied by flashing strobe lights for the hearing impaired. The shoppers who'd been approaching her end of the mall stopped in their tracks. Waving her arms, she signaled for them to go back the way they'd come. They turned and did so, confused, but obedient.

It was working! She'd done it! She could barely hear herself think, but she'd done it. The bank robber wasn't bound to appreciate it very much, but who cared what *he* thought? She'd saved innocent people from getting caught up in an armed bank heist. Just like the Night Hunter would have done!

She glanced at Overton's to see what Angela was doing, but there was no sign of her. Still hiding behind the register counter. Well, that was all right, as long as she'd let emergency services know what was going on. Inside Eastport Bank, everyone was lying on the floor with their hands over their heads. They all appeared to be breathing. Nina hadn't heard any gunshots. There was no sign of the robber. Nina assumed he was wherever the money was, stuffing it into his pockets or whatever bags he'd brought along. As long as help came soon, she didn't—

That's when the arm—rock hard, like iron—clamped around her throat, and she was dragged backward until she was pressed up against a long, muscular body. Something small and circular was held against her temple.

This, Nina realized, just wasn't her day.

"Are you the one who set off that damned alarm?" a hoarse voice rasped close beside her ear.

Nina flinched. She didn't need to turn her head to know who had grabbed hold of her. She could see a bit of red clown fluff sticking out past the mask from the corner of one eye. Just like she could see the gun he was pressing to her head.

"Yes," she managed to croak. It was hard to talk with the man in the trench coat's arm pressing so tightly against her throat. She'd instinctively thrown up both hands in order to try to pull that arm away, but it was no use. It was like trying to move a two-ton boulder. "You'd better get out of here. The police are on their way."

She hoped.

"Not without a hostage," Clown Mask hissed. It was kind of hard to hear him over the whooping of the fire alarm. But his mouth was so close to her ear, she could feel his hot breath singeing her skin.

"You really don't want to take me as your hostage," Nina advised him. "I'd make a terrible hostage."

"Yeah?" Clown Mask sounded amused. "Who do you suggest I take instead? One of your friends from inside the bank?"

Nina shook her head, her heart pounding. Not Katie. She had that new baby. And not Rick, either. He had a heart condition and kids at home, too.

"What about your friend in the dress shop there, huh?" Clown Mask breathed. He was pushing her as he spoke . . . pushing her down the concourse, past Overton's, where she could see the top of Angela's head, peeking out over the counter, the telephone still clutched to one ear. "Should we go in there and swap you for her? Would you like that better, huh?"

"No," Nina said, sullenly. Whatever Clown Mask had

planned for her—and Nina didn't kid herself that it was going to be anything too pleasant—Angela wouldn't last a minute. And if she herself happened to live through it—and Nina wasn't betting she was going to—it would scar her way less than it would Angela.

Because Angela—whose loving parents only made her work this single weekend shift at their shop to teach her responsibility—had never known hardship in her life. Except the hardship of having not been invited to Lauren van der Waals's party.

Nina hoped Angela would have a very nice time there without her.

"I didn't think so," Clown Mask said, with a low sound in his throat that Nina could only assume was a chuckle. He continued to push her along past the waterfall, toward the side exits.

They burst through the twin doors together, and Nina was greeted with a blast of cold night air in her face—air that was only going to get colder since she didn't have a coat on—and the welcome relief of no more fire alarm sound.

She was also greeted by the wail of a police siren as a squad car skidded to a halt in the parking lot in front of them. *Someone* had gotten through to emergency services, at least.

Clown Mask, who'd loosened his grip on her throat only slightly, now tightened it. A young police officer flung himself out from behind the wheel and, using the car as a shield, pointed his service revolver at them.

"Stay where you are," he yelled, his voice strangely soft after the loudness of the alarm inside. "Put down your weapon, nice and slow."

"I have a better idea," Clown Mask said to the police officer. "You put down *your* weapon, or I'll blow a hole in this girl's head. How about that?"

The police officer, who looked barely old enough to have graduated from high school, let alone the academy, seemed confused. Nina could hear other sirens in the distance, but it sounded like it would be a while before they got anywhere close.

"That's what I thought," Clown Mask said, sounding smug. "Now, this young lady and I are going to walk over to my car, real slow, and you're going to let us. Or like I said, I'll splatter her brains all over the front doors of Calder Mall. And I don't think your chief would like it if I did that. Do you?"

The cop said nothing. He continued to keep his gun pointed at them, however, as Clown Mask dragged her toward his getaway car, a beat-up four-door sedan parked illegally along the curb right next to where they'd been standing. If there'd actually been a cop patrolling the mall's parking lot, he'd have gotten a ticket and been towed.

But all the cops were busy on the far side of town, trying to stop real crimes—the kind of crimes the Night Hunter had finally gotten so sick of reading about in the paper, he'd put on a mask and decided to go and fight them himself.

And now look what was happening over at the mall.

"Listen," Nina said in a low voice to her captor. "Let me go now. He won't shoot you. He's too scared. And you'll make better time without me."

"Nice try, sweetie," Clown Mask said with a chuckle. "Now get in the car."

Nina knew the last thing she ought to do was get inside that car.

But from the way she'd seen him push Katie down back in the bank, she also knew that he wasn't going to be shy about using that gun . . . even with a cop standing a few dozen yards away.

She let him shove her into the passenger seat of the sedan. *It's all right*, she told herself. *I'll jump out when we slow down to take a corner.*

It would hurt, but it would be better than whatever waited for her at the end of this.

Then Clown Mask was in the driver's seat, one hand on the wheel while the other continued to point the gun at her head. As they took off, his tires spun in the bits of sand left over from a recent snowfall. Nina barely had time to buckle her seat belt before he accelerated. He laughed bitterly at this, as if to say she had more important things to worry about than being in a car crash, which she supposed was true.

Then, with a spray of sand and gravel, the sedan careened from the parking lot, heading down 95 and away from the mall, the lights of which grew faint in the distance. Nina held on to her seat belt, conscious of the gun still pointed to her temple. *Not yet,* she told herself. *Soon. He has to slow down sometime.* And then she'd jump. And run for all she was worth.

"You're never going to make it," she told Clown Mask as he swerved to merge into evening traffic. She was sure no one suspected that they were slowing down for a psychotic bank robber.

Clown Mask just chuckled. "In this town? With these cops? Watch me."

He had a point. Eastport's police department was stretched to the limit, with barely enough men and women to cover routine patrols, let alone any additional emergencies that might occur. The city was bankrupt, and the mayor, in his infinite wisdom, had cut back on city workers first. The police department had been the first to see major layoffs.

"I'll be home counting my payoff before *Jeopardy!*" Clown Mask said, with a sneer.

"And what about me?" Nina asked, in a tight voice. She knew she wasn't going to like his answer. Still, she was hoping he'd lie to her.

He didn't.

"You?" He used the mouth of the pistol to push back some of her dark hair so he could get a better look at her face. "You, I'm starting to like."

Oh, no, thought Nina. They were going eighty miles an hour down the fast lane. There was no way she could jump out at this speed and survive. And death, to Nina, did not seem preferable to the alternative at this point. There still might be opportunities for escape when they got to his house, or wherever they were going. There was still hope. He liked her—or thought she was pretty, or whatever. She could get out of this, if she played her cards right. She could still get out of this.

There was still a chance she might live.

"What the hell?" Clown Mask asked a second later, abruptly removing the gun from her hair and glancing urgently into the rearview mirror.

Nina looked back but couldn't see what was alarming him. She'd hoped to see the red glare of police sirens, but instead she saw only the single headlight of a motorcycle. True, it seemed to be tailgating them. But that wasn't anything to get upset about.

Then she remembered:

He rides alone/Just a rolling stone.

The Night Hunter was rumored to ride a motorcycle sometimes. Other times—at least according to eyewitnesses, who swore they weren't making it up—he drove some kind of armored vehicle, like an SUV tank.

But it was too much to hope that the Night Hunter had somehow managed to find them—out of all the cars on the interstate—when even the cops hadn't been able to. Nina swallowed down the sudden hope that had swelled inside her. She had experienced far too much disappointment in recent months to allow her spirits to be crushed that way again. There was only one person in this life, she knew, who you could count on . . . one. And that was yourself. If she was going to get out of this, she would have to do it on her own.

"This guy's riding my ass," Clown Mask muttered, switching lanes abruptly.

But Nina could tell by the high beam in the rearview

mirror and the loud roar behind them that the move had done no good.

"What's with this guy?" Clown Mask demanded, and switched lanes again.

The motorcycle stayed right behind him, the roar from its engine seeming to envelop them, reverberating in Nina's chest.

Nina couldn't help it. She began to feel hopeful. It was an emotion she hadn't allowed herself to feel in a long, long time.

"Maybe," she said, "it's the Night Hunter."

"What?" Clown Mask asked distractedly as he tried to make his way back to the passing lane.

"You know," Nina said. "The Night Hunter. That vigilante who's been making citizen's arrests of criminals the cops haven't been able—or had time—to arrest. He left that crime boss Vincent Gamboni tied up in his own car by the docks last week, along with a boatload of seven hundred thousand dollars' worth of stolen goods. You're kind of small potatoes," Nina added, "compared to him. But then, you are adding kidnapping to grand larceny, which are both felonies."

"Shut the hell up," Clown Mask said, pushing a button to bring the driver's side window down.

"I'm just saying," Nina said, "a known drug dealer who's been wanted for murder and aggravated assault and on the run for three years? The Night Hunter found him and brought him in with no shots fired. He's that good. And you think you're going to get away? In your little clown mask?" Nina laughed. She couldn't help it.

Which was when Clown Mask leaned out the driver's side window and fired a shot behind them, in the direction of the relentlessly pursuing motorcycle.

The sound of the report was so loud that Nina screamed and flung both hands over her ears.

"What are you doing?" she shrieked. "Are you trying to get us both killed?"

"Drive," Clown Mask said. Only he'd ripped off his mask in order to take better aim at his prey, and now Nina could see his irregular features: the badly reset broken nose; the too-small, beady eyes, blinking at her with a glint of desperation. "I'm going to kill this bastard. Take the wheel."

Before Nina had time to regret what she'd said— she'd only meant to scare him, after all—her captor had slithered halfway out the driver's side window and was unloading his pistol in the direction of the man on the motorcycle.

If she didn't want them to careen into the cars on

either side of them, Nina had no choice but to seize the wheel of the car and slam her foot on the gas.

But since she could no more allow him to kill the Night Hunter than she could allow him to kill her, she yanked violently on the wheel, swerving right. And then, praying to a God she wasn't entirely sure she believed in anymore, she cut across three lanes of traffic. Horns blared as cars veered out of their way, barely missing them.

"What the hell are you doing?" her captor slithered back inside the car to shout at her. He seized the wheel, wrestling it from her grasp.

But Nina wouldn't give up. She gave it another violent tug while pressing down with all her might on the gas, aiming the car for a copse of trees she could see rushing toward them from the darkness alongside the road. All the while she was praying, *Please don't let me die, please don't let me die, please don't let me die. . . .*

Clown Mask responded by striking her hard against the side of her head with the butt of his gun. Instinctively, she released the wheel and let go of the gas, seizing the side of her face and recoiling in pain and confusion as her vision swam in blackness.

When her eyesight cleared a split second later, she experienced several agonizingly long moments of clarity as the car zoomed off the highway, bounced over the shoulder, and dove into the trees toward which she'd aimed it. She only had time to fling up both arms in a useless attempt to protect her head before the car landed with a stunningly hard force, a deafening crunch of metal, and a splinter of shattering glass.

And this time when the blackness came, it consumed her.

When Nina opened her eyes, she heard the sound of cars passing in the distance, and somewhere closer by, the gentle cascade of running water. Her head ached, and it took a few seconds for her vision to focus. When it finally did, the first thing she saw was a pair of blue eyes staring at her from a field of darkness. At first she thought she must be in a cave, or a movie theater. Why else would it be so dark?

Then she realized that it was nighttime, and she was outside. There was something warm over her body, but her face felt the chill, and so did the places where her body connected with the cold, hard ground.

She also realized that the reason the blue eyes appeared to be looking at her from a field of darkness was that they were peering at her from behind two holes. The man kneeling beside her was wearing a black rubber mask.

She gave a start, and the man—who, she realized, was cradling her upper body, trying to keep her head supported—said, in a low voice that was more rasp than whisper, "An ambulance is on the way. You're going to be all right. Just keep still."

Nina wasn't sure she believed him. She hurt all over. She tried moving her legs—it would be just her luck if she turned out to be paralyzed—and was relieved to find that she could bend both her knees with some effort.

"Hey," the man with the black mask rasped, sounding as if he were laughing a little. "I thought I said to keep still."

Which was all well and good for him to say. But he hadn't been in that car with a gun pointed to his head a few minutes (had it only been minutes?) ago.

"Wh-where is he?" Nina demanded, turning her head. Big mistake. Waves of pain shot through it.

"He's gone," the man in the mask said. Another man in a mask, Nina thought, with a groan. Too many masks for one night. "Don't worry about him. You're safe now."

Nina couldn't see the wreckage of Clown Mask's car. But she could smell it, the acrid smoke filling the night air.

"Is he . . . dead?" she asked, hopefully.

"No," he said, and again there was a chuckle in his

voice. "He can't have gotten far. Once help comes for you, I'll look for him."

Nina tensed. "You should go. You should look for him now, before he gets away. Don't worry about me, I'll be all right."

"Hey," her rescuer said, laughing now. "You put your life on the line for me back there. Hanging with you until the ambulance comes is the least I can do, Nina."

She blinked, trying to remember. Had she saved his life? Oh, right. The Night Hunter. Clown Mask had been shooting at him, and she'd steered the car into the trees. The Night Hunter must have pulled her from the burning car, and he was here with her, now, waiting for the ambulance. She had finally met him. Only—

"How," she said, blinking with confusion, "do you know my name?"

He didn't say anything for a beat.

"Your wallet," he said. "Sorry. I looked through it. I wanted to know to whom I owed my life."

"How did you know?" she asked. "About me? That I was in the car with . . . him?"

"I heard about the kidnapping over the police scanner," he said. "I picked the two of you up as he merged onto Ninety-five. It was pretty easy. You were the only ones going a hundred miles an hour. That was brave, what you did. Driving the car into the trees when he started shooting."

"He was . . . he said he was going to take me with him," Nina said. She didn't want to go into detail. Looking into those blue eyes—as cold as the air around her—she could see that she didn't have to. The mouth beneath the formfitting rubber mask, the only part of him that wasn't swathed in black, set into a firm line. He knew. He knew exactly what she meant.

The pain in her head was pulsating. The smoke from the burning car seemed to have seared her lungs, though she knew he'd pulled her away in time. Finally, Nina added, "Besides, he was shooting at you. You're not bulletproof . . ." She thought of the song. " . . . are you?"

"Sort of," he said, and tapped his chest, which made a strange echoing sound. "Kevlar body armor. So, next time, don't ram into any trees on my account. No need. Though I do appreciate it."

His mouth twisted into a grin, convincing Nina that without the mask, he'd be handsome. Handsome, but also frightening—there was a considerable breadth of shoulder beneath the black body armor, not to mention the fact that his chest seemed about half a mile wide.

Still. For a moment, Nina saw something warm in those icy blue eyes.

And then she heard the siren and saw the red-and-white flash.

"Looks like your ride's here," he said, and she could feel him gently lowering her head. "I've got to go. I'm not particularly well liked by the local authorities. Besides, I have to go look for the driver of this illegally parked vehicle over here and have a few words with him."

"Wait," Nina said, her heart speeding up.

"You'll be all right, Nina," he assured her, squeezing her hand. "I've left flares so they'll know how to find you."

"Not that," Nina said. She could feel the darkness closing in again, but she fought against it. "Who are you? I don't even know."

"Oh," he said, with a smile, as voices sounded in the thick tangle of woods around them. "I think we'll see each other again."

And then he was gone, just as the first emergency service worker stepped into the clearing into which he'd carried her, and cried, "Miss? It's all right, miss, we're here now."

For a few minutes Nina wasn't sure he'd ever even been there. She thought she might have imagined the whole thing.

Except that later, as they were loading her onto the ambulance, one of the EMS workers lifted the edges of the thick black blanket that had been wrapped so securely around her, and asked, "Where did this come from? It's not one of ours."

And then Nina saw, at the same time that everyone else on the scene did, that it wasn't a blanket at all.

"That's a cape," said one of the ambulance drivers.

"You don't think—" one of the firemen began, but another cut him off.

"Don't start."

"We weren't the first on the scene," said another. "Someone pulled her out of the car, stopped her bleeding, and laid those flares."

Nina would have told them. She would have said who it was, and gladly.

But she was too busy thinking about something else. One of the EMTs had asked her for her ID, and when she'd reached for her wallet, she realized she'd left it back at the mall, along with her purse, her cell phone, and everything else she'd brought with her to work that night.

So the Night Hunter had lied about how he'd known her name. He'd known her name because he'd known *her*. He'd known her because . . .

. . . she knew him. They'd met before.

Of course. Those eyes. Those icy blue eyes from all those photos in the newspaper. Those blue eyes that, far into their depths, had hidden wells of warmth.

She'd know them anywhere.

And he was right: They would be seeing each other soon. Tomorrow night, at Lauren van der Waals's party.

And this time, Nina wouldn't feel weird about walking up and saying hi.

TUITION

· WALTER SORRELLS ·

Marlon's phone vibrated as the third tumbler clicked.

He looked at his phone. It was Mom. Great.

He thumbed the green button. "What," he whispered, still twisting the knob on the safe with his other hand.

"It's your mother. Couldn't you be a little more polite when you answer the phone?"

"I know who it *is*," he whispered. "What do you want? I'm kinda busy here." He glanced at his watch. Eight thirty-seven. Time was running out. It was an antique Mosler Model 37B, the kind they used in banks back in the old days. In a perfect world he would have drilled it.

But drills made too much noise. The place where they were doing the job—the headquarters of International Logicorp—was patrolled by well-trained security guards and protected by all kinds of motion sensors and sound sensors and heat detectors . . .

"My book club's running late," his mom said. "You think you can pick up your brother from chess team practice?"

Marlon sighed. "Mom, I'm *busy!*"

"Doing what? Doing *what?*"

"Okay okay okay okay okay," he hissed. Among the other important things that she didn't remember about today, apparently she didn't even remember that he was on a job. "I'll get Ray-Ray. God!"

Marlon closed his phone, wiped his brow on his sleeve. Chess team! For godsake.

His fingers were cramped and tired from slowly twisting the dial on the safe. He was monitoring the sound of the mechanism through earphones. But he also had an electronic monitor with a little gauge on it that twitched at the tiniest sound. The Mosler was a beautifully made safe, old-school craftsmanship, with amazingly quiet tumblers. Only a real master could crack it by ear.

"Who was that?" Irving said.

"Can we be quiet, Irving?" Marlon said. "I'm trying to concentrate."

"Whatever." Irving was a tall old guy, like forty or fifty, who sat on the desk swinging his legs aimlessly. Marlon wasn't sure why his father had sent Irving along on this job. Marlon could have done this one by himself.

Marlon waggled his fingers, trying to get the kinks out, then began working on the safe again, slowly twisting the dial. He was close now. One more number and they could get the stuff and get out of here.

After a few minutes Irving hissed, "Hey. Guards!"

Marlon clicked off his flashlight and froze, his heart going into overdrive. The guards were only supposed to come around once an hour! Had somebody tipped them off?

The footsteps grew closer and closer. There were two of them, talking. That was a good sign. If they had been tipped off, they'd have their guns out and would be moving silently. Still . . .

The footsteps stopped. He could see two shadows in the band of light that came through the crack underneath the door. They were standing right in front of the office, not fifteen feet from where he was crouched!

His dad had assured him this was going to be a big

score. If he pulled this one off, his dad swore that he wouldn't have to do any of this crap again. This one job would pay for college, the full ride.

Marlon had been admitted to Princeton in the fall. But the financial aid didn't cover everything. Even after the loans and the grants, he was going to have to come up with eighteen grand every single year. Eighteen grand! How could anybody afford the place?

Outside the room, one of the guards said, "What's that? Did you leave that there?"

"No," the other guard said. "It wasn't here before."

"You sure?"

"Of course I'm sure."

"Well, open the door, you idiot. Something's not right here."

"I don't have the keys."

"I thought you had the keys."

"I thought *you* had the keys!"

"Do I have to do everything around here?"

The two guards walked away, bad-mouthing each other. They didn't sound very worried.

But still. He wasn't sure what they'd seen out there in the hallway. Maybe Irving left something out there. The guy was so sloppy. Marlon never could figure out why his father kept Irving on in his crew. Marlon's dad was the kind of guy who always made sure every detail was right. *Every* detail.

Bing! The elevator bell sounded. Then the elevator doors closed and the voices of the two security guards disappeared.

"We gotta clear out, kid," Irving said. "They're onto us."

Marlon felt sick. He was close. *So* close!

"No. I'm almost there."

"Kid, your old man'll kill me if I let you get pinched."

"No!" Marlon kept working the dial, eyes glued to the gauge on the monitor.

"Whaddaya mean, *no*?"

"That's my tuition in there. That's my ticket out of this crap!"

"Crap? You know what your old man went through to teach you everything you know? Safes? Explosives? Locks? Alarms? Your family has been in this business for three generations. Your old man is a master. You lucky little punk, he's already taught you more than I learned in—"

"Shh!"

Marlon kept turning the knob. He wanted to rush. But he knew you couldn't rush a thing like this. Irving was right about one thing, his father *had* taught him well. At age sixteen Marlon knew more about safecracking than most people learned in a lifetime. All those hours his father had drilled him, tested him, taught him. The shortcuts, the techniques.

It all comes down to intuition, though, his father always said. *Some got it, some don't. And, son—you've got it.* It used to make his heart swell with pleasure when his father said stuff like that.

But now? Now it made him all queasy and sick. He just wanted to go to college like a normal teenager. All this sneaking around and breaking into places had seemed fun when he was a kid, with no worries about jail or anything. But today was his birthday. Strictly speaking, he turned seventeen in . . . well . . . in less than an hour. Which meant that by the time he finished this job, he'd be old enough to get sent up to the Big House. Grown-up jail, bro, that was no joke.

Irving started pacing up and down, staring at the stopwatch. He knew exactly how long it would take for the guards to get back. Everything had been timed down to the last second. It was a two-minute-and-twenty-second walk from the security office down on Floor B to the office they were in. Round-trip—four minutes, forty seconds.

His phone rang. Mom again.

"Jeez!" he said.

"It's your mother," his mother said.

"I know! What!"

"Ray-Ray just called. He's standing outside the school right now. How *could* you?"

Crap. He'd forgotten all about Ray-Ray. "I'll be there soon, Mom. God!"

"You're so touchy today! Why are you so touchy?"

He hung up.

Why was he so touchy? *Because you forgot my birthday, Mom. You and Dad and Ray-Ray, you all forgot my birthday.* Seventeen. The big one. Here he was cracking a Mosler 37B in the executive boardroom of International Logi-corp when any normal kid would be at the frickin' Olive Garden, shoveling a big plate of pasta in their face and opening presents while all their normal friends sat around laughing and joking, without a care in the world.

It wasn't right.

Chess team. Man, that chafed his ass. Had *Marlon* ever gotten a chance to be on the chess team? Or play Little League? Or be in a school play? *Hell* no! All these years his father had been pushing him and pushing and pushing him, training him night and day, making him memorize a million locks and safes and alarm system schematics, building special tools in the machine shop, practicing his lock-picking skills—it never ended! *Oh, Marlon, you're so smart and talented and blah blah blah blah blah!* All these expectations, all this pressure. It wasn't fair! It was like it never occurred to the old man that a kid might want to be something other than a freakin' master criminal.

Ray-Ray, on the other hand, never got pushed at all. He came home, he did his homework, he went to chess club or whatever, and nobody gave a crap that he couldn't open a safe to save his life. What a spoiled little brat. It was enough to make Marlon puke.

"How long?" Marlon whispered. The gauge on the scope hadn't budged.

"Two forty-five," Irving said tensely.

"Do the Tisdale," Marlon said.

"Huh?"

"The Tisdale! Do the Tisdale! It might give me another two minutes."

"Or it might make them suspicious."

"Just do it! This is my frickin' tuition in here."

"Your what?"

"College! It's my college tuition!"

Irving stared at him liked he'd just fallen out of the sky. "College? What are you talking about, college?"

"I'm going to college. Princeton. What's so frickin' bizarre about that?"

"You make me sad, kid. What's Princeton gonna do for you? Teach you to be some kind of stuck-up jerk in a gray suit, is what." He looked at the stopwatch. "Two-oh-five."

"Make the call! God!"

Irving pulled out his phone, hit the speed dial button. "Yes, hi, security?" he said, doing a perfect imitation of a woman's voice. A very sexy woman. "I'm a little embarrassed. This is Miss Tisdale in accounting. I worked late today, and gosh, I'm just terrified of the parking garage at this time of the evening. I swear the other day there was a man lurking down there. Lurking! Yes, lurking." Irving nodded his head, getting into his little act. "Could you? Oh, I just hate to trouble you. But it would really . . . yes . . . yes. You're *so* sweet. I know. I know. You're *so* sweet. I'll meet you at the elevator on the first floor in two minutes. Byyyyeeeee!"

"Scary," Marlon said. "You're way too good at that."

"At least I'm not going to Princeton. Jesus H.— couldn't you at least go to Pitt, Ohio State, Michigan, someplace with a football team?"

"Princeton has a football team!"

"Pffff!" Irving said, waving his hand dismissively. "Forty-eight seconds."

Marlon kept working the dial. If the Tisdale had worked and both the security guys went to the elevator on one, it would buy them five or ten minutes. If not . . .

He knew he was close. In the end safecracking came down to mathematics. You turned the dial at a certain rate, you had to hit the number after a certain amount of time.

Marlon had a sinking feeling. Maybe he was just never going to get this safe open. He should have been at Olive Garden opening presents.

It used to be that every birthday his mom and dad would tell the story about the day he was born. They'd go back and forth, interrupting each other in their enthusiasm for the story—all about how it had been a beautiful fall day, the crisp air, the leaves turning, all this junk, and how her water broke in the middle of a job and how she and Dad had to go racing to the hospital with all the loot in the trunk of the car. He was doing ninety right through the middle of town when a cop had pulled them over for speeding. But then, when Marlon's dad had told the cop that his wife was having a baby, the cop put on his siren and led them right to the hospital. If the guy had only known they had a hundred and ten thousand bucks' worth of stolen antique silver in the trunk! They'd gotten to the hospital at 9:03 on the dot, Marlon's hairy little head popping out right there in the lobby of the hospital.

Well, apparently the story wasn't interesting to Mom and Dad anymore.

They had totally, totally forgotten. Not only was there no story—there was no card, no Olive Garden, no present at the breakfast table. Nada. Bubkes.

It sucked.

"Fifteen seconds," Irving said. "I'm clearing out of here."

"I'm almost there. I can feel it."

"Hey, kid, you can afford to get popped. You'll just go to juvie. Me, this is my third strike."

Marlon looked at his watch. "Five more minutes and I'm legal," he said.

"Huh?" Irving's eyebrows went up. "Hold on, you saying today's your—"

"Yeah, today's my—"

Bing!

He glanced up. It was the sound of the elevator reaching their floor.

Dammit! His college tuition! It was right there. A normal life was right there on the other side of that safe, not six inches from his fingers. He was so *close!* He was sure he'd have it in seconds.

He hesitated. His heart was banging away in his chest and his limbs were trembling. His finger twitched.

And that tiny tremor was enough.

The little gauge on the scope flickered. The last tumbler had dropped!

Marlon grinned. "Got it!" he said triumphantly.

As he grabbed the handle to pull open the safe, he could hear the sound of the elevator doors opening. Frantically, he yanked at the handle. The door must have weighed three hundred pounds. It moved slowly, slowly on its oiled hinges.

The elevators were about fifty yards from the executive offices. There was still a distant chance they could get away.

"Light!" Marlon hissed.

Irving hesitated, then flicked on his flashlight, directing it at the safe. Marlon kept pulling on the handle, the door yawning slowly open.

The footsteps were growing closer and closer and closer.

He could almost taste it now. Inside the safe was a stack of very specialized computer chips, each one of them worth twenty-four thousand bucks on the black market. His cut of the take would pay for four years of Princeton. He wouldn't have to crack another safe, cut another fence, nitro another lock—nothing.

And then he could have a normal life. Be an accountant or a salesman or a middle manager at a life insurance company. He could be anything!

The door swung all the way open.

The footsteps halted. Keys jingled. He glanced over, saw the shadow underneath the door.

He looked back at the safe.

And a wave of sadness and horror swept through him. Except for a manila folder that lay at the bottom like some neglected piece of trash, it was utterly and completely empty.

All this for nothing!

Outside, the key slid into the lock. Marlon shook his head. It was all over.

He glanced at his watch.

He was seventeen now. He had been eligible to serve hard time in the Big House for one minute and thirty-eight seconds.

He wanted to cry.

Irving's light flicked off as the door began to open.

Marlon couldn't even move. He knelt there, staring into the black empty safe. All his hopes and dreams, gone. Normal life, gone. Princeton, gone.

"Surprise!"

The lights flicked on.

Marlon whipped around.

Suddenly people were coming from everywhere, crowding out of the closets and the cabinets and the executive bathroom.

"Happy birthday!"

Marlon fell to his knees.

His father, grinning like a Cheshire cat, was walking into the room, followed by his mother, who carried a cake with seventeen candles on it.

Ray-Ray was walking out of the bathroom.

His friends Jerry and Justin and several members of his father's crew—they were appearing from everywhere.

Marlon put his hands over his face. "God, you guys!" he said. "You scared the crap out of me! I can't believe it. I thought you forgot my birthday."

Marlon's father laughed loudly and gave him a hug.

"Come on," his mother said. "You think we'd forget *this* day?"

"I don't know," Marlon said.

"I can remember the day you were born like it was yesterday," she said.

"We were on a job . . ." his father said.

"It was a crisp fall day . . ."

". . . and the leaves were turning . . ."

Marlon gratefully let them tell the same old story. The cop who pulled them over, the antique silver in the trunk, the siren, the lobby of the hospital . . . A wave of relief and comfort swept through him.

"So this was all a setup, huh?" Marlon said. "I opened that safe and it was stone empty. I about had a heart attack."

"Empty?" his father said.

Marlon squinted at him. "Yeah. Nothing there."

His father walked over to the safe, reached in, pulled out the folder lying in the bottom. "No, son. It's not empty."

Marlon looked curiously at his father's face. He was smiling broadly

"Son, I've been saving for years." His smile faded a little. "You know for a while it made me sad to see that your heart wasn't in this business. You have such *talent*! And it hurt me a little to think that you were going to squander it all. You could have been one of the great ones." He sighed. "But you know what? You don't go into crime for the money. You do it because you love it. It's a calling." Marlon's father spread his hands. "Son, I just want you to be happy."

He handed Marlon the manila folder he'd just taken out of the safe.

Marlon looked at it blankly.

"Open it, son."

Marlon opened the folder. Inside was a slim document It said:

·PRINCETON UNIVERSITY·
OFFICE OF FINANCIAL AID
Prepayment Plan

"Four years, kid," Marlon's father said. "Paid in full."

Marlon's jaw dropped. "You mean this . . ." He made a gesture with his hands, taking in the whole office, the Mosler 37B, the folder, the circle of friends and family.

"All a setup. Last night when I said I was going down to watch the ponies? I broke in here and planted this document." He clapped Marlon on the shoulder. "This is it, kid. You're done. Last job. You're a citizen now."

His father looked at his watch, clapped his hands

sharply. "All right, guys, we've had our fun. It's nine fifteen. The security guards will be back in seven minutes. We gotta get out of here."

Marlon was beaming. "I can't believe it. This was so perfect. The safe. The locks. The security guards in the hallway. I bought the whole thing."

His father looked at him quizzically. "Security guards? What security guards?"

"That wasn't you? In the hallway? Pretending to be security guards?"

Everyone in the room went silent.

The footsteps in the hallway and the sirens in the parking lot outside went off at the exact same moment that the burglar alarm began to blare.

Within seconds the room was full of police officers, screaming and pointing guns. "Everybody down on the ground! Down on the ground, now!"

It was over in seconds.

Marlon lay on his stomach, a wave of darkness washing over him as the policeman put a knee in his back and cuffed him.

"What's your name, kid?"

Marlon said nothing.

The cop pulled out his wallet, looked at his driver's

license. "Hey, look at this!" the cop said. "Scumbag here just turned seventeen."

Marlon lay motionless. The Princeton University financial aid document lay on the floor near his face. A second cop walked by, laughing. His black boot trampling on the financial aid document, ripping the pages apart, and leaving a black shoe print on the torn paper.

"Happy birthday, kid!" the cop said, hoisting him to his feet. "Happy birthday!"

TAGGER

· JAMES ROLLINS ·

With a practiced flip of her wrist, Soo-ling Choi shook the spray can and applied the final trail of red paint against the cement wall of the dark alley. Finished, she took a step back to examine her handiwork, careful not to get any paint on her black silk dress.

She wasn't entirely happy with the result. She'd done better. It was the Chinese symbol known as *fu*, her signature mark. Only sixteen, she continued to be highly critical of herself. She knew she was talented. She'd even been accepted for early enrollment at the L.A. Academy of Design. But this was more important than any scholarship.

She checked her watch. Auntie Loo would already be at the theater. She scowled at the mark.

It'll have to do.

Reaching out, she touched the center of the Chinese glyph. As usual, she felt the familiar tingling that made her joints burn. The warmth spread up her arm and enveloped her in a dizzying wash. The glyph glowed for a breath, pushing back the dark shadows of the alley.

Done.

Before she could break contact with the symbol, an icy-cold pain tore at her wrist like talons. It seared deep, down to the bone. With a gasp, she ripped her arm away and stumbled back.

Ow . . . what the heck was that?

She examined her wrist. It was unmarked, but an echo of that cold touch remained. She rubbed her arm, trying to melt the ice away, and studied her work with narrowed eyes.

On the wall, her bright crimson mark had gone black, darker than the shadows of the alley.

She continued to massage her wrist, bending it one way, then the other, struggling to figure out what had happened. The symbolic glyph—her "tag" for the past three years—was exactly like the hundreds she had plastered throughout the greater Los Angeles area.

Did I do something wrong? Did I draw it too fast, too sloppily, make some dreadful mistake?

Worry grew to an ache in her chest. She considered redrawing it, but she had no more time. The curtain for the ballet would be rising in less than five minutes. Auntie Loo would already be in the family's private box. With little patience for frivolity, her aunt would be furious if Soo-ling was late again.

As the pain subsided in her arm, the shadows seemed to drain out of the paint. The crimson richness of the *fu* symbol returned, as if nothing had happened.

Whatever the problem had been, it seemed to be gone now. She shoved the spray can into her messenger bag and hurried down the alley toward the waiting limousine.

She shot one last glance over her shoulder as she reached for the door handle. The symbolic character still shone on the wall like a splash of blood. To most Chinese, it was merely a blessing of good fortune associated with celebrations of the New Year. It represented two hands placing a jar of rice wine on an altar as an offering.

But for Soo-ling, the painted character of *fu* was power, a ward of protection wherever she painted it. There would be no robbery at this location tonight; the proprietor of this 7-Eleven would be safe.

Or so she allowed herself to imagine. It was a small way she honored her dead mother and her ancient superstitions. A way to stay connected to her, to a past that both mother and daughter shared that went back centuries, to villages nestled amid rice paddies, to mornings fragrant with cherry blossoms.

She cast up a silent prayer to her mother and climbed into the back of the limo. A gust of sea breeze from nearby Huntington Beach wafted inside, tinged with just a hint of salt—and an underlying trace of rot. A shiver shook through her.

Just fish and algae, she assured herself.

Behind the wheel, Charles nodded to her. They didn't need words. He had been with her family for as long as she could remember.

Wanting a moment of privacy, she raised the glass partition between them and tried to compose herself. Her reflection hovered in the window before her. Her long black hair had been coiled into a precarious pile atop her head, the cascade held at bay by a pair of emerald-capped hairpins. Her eyes matched the pins in color and shine.

Like a ghost of Mother.

Over the past few years, Soo-ling could not help but notice that she was slowly growing into her mother's image, one generation becoming another. An ache of loneliness and loss hollowed her out.

She went back to that final bedside visit with her mother before the malignant lymphoma stole her away. The hospital room had smelled of bleach and rubbing alcohol, no place for her fragile mother, who believed in herbal tea remedies, the healing power of statues and symbols, and ancient superstitions.

"This is passed to you, *si low chai*, my child," her mother had whispered, sliding a sheet of hospital stationery toward her. "It is our family's heritage, passed from mothers to daughters for thirteen generations. You are of the thirteenth generation, and this is the thirteenth year of your birth. This number has power."

"Mother, rest please. The chemotherapy is very taxing. You need your sleep."

Soo-ling had taken the sheet of paper from her mother

and turned it over. In a beautiful cursive script, her mother had drawn the Chinese character for good fortune.

Fu.

"My little rose, you are now the guardian of the City of Angels," she said with a mix of pride and sorrow, struggling to breathe each word. "I wish I could have explained earlier. These mysteries can only be revealed after the first blood of womanhood."

"Mother, please . . . rest . . ."

Her mother continued, her eyes glazed by both memory and drugs. She told stories of prophetic dreams and the power to block curses with the proper stroke of paint on a wall or door. Soo-ling had obediently listened, but she also noted the bleat of the heart monitor, the drip of the IV line, the whisper of a television down the hall.

What place did all these ancient stories full of ghosts and gods have in the modern world of electrocardiograms, needle biopsies, and insurance forms?

Finally, a nurse whisked into the room on rubber-soled shoes. "Visiting hours are over, Ms. Choi."

Her mother began to protest, but a quick kiss from Soo-ling calmed her. "I'll be back tomorrow . . . after school."

Glad for the excuse, Soo-ling fled the room, relieved to

escape not just the stories but the demon named cancer. Still, her mother had called after her. "You must beware the—" But the closing door cut off those last words, silencing her forever.

That night, her mother had slipped into a coma and died.

Soo-ling remembered staring down at the hospital stationery clutched in her hands.

Blessing and luck, she thought. A lot of good it did her mother.

"We've arrived, Ms. Choi," Charles said, drawing her out of the past as he pulled the limo to the curb in front of the theater in Santa Monica.

Soo-ling shook herself out of her reverie and slid across the seat. The driver already had the door open. "Thank you, Charles."

As she climbed out, an anxious teenager in a rented tuxedo tripped down the steps toward her. "Soo! About time you got here!"

A smile filled her at the sight of him, but she did not let it reach her face. It was not proper for a Chinese girl to show strong emotions. Like casting her symbol, it was another way to honor her mother, to adhere to tradition in this small way.

The young man rushed up to her. He stood a head

taller than her, gangly in the overlarge tuxedo. His long hair had been pulled back into a ponytail.

Bobby Tomlinson was her age. He'd been her friend since kindergarten. One of her few. Both misfits growing up, they had banded together. He was a computer geek and film buff, and she was the shy student who never spoke above a whisper. Over time they had grown to share a secret love of tagging. He had introduced her to it when she was eleven, and she was instantly hooked. It became an outlet for rebellion against the world as her mother became sick, a sliver of freedom and joy that helped Soo-ling cope with her overwhelming grief and anger. Over the next years, they ran the streets together, dodging police, struggling to leave their mark on the city in multicolored splashes of paint.

The smile trapped inside her grew larger with the memory. Bobby led her up the steps and inside. He babbled on in a rush about his new intern position at Titan Pictures.

"We start shooting tomorrow on that vampire musical I was telling you about. I'll be helping with the gaffing crew!"

She glanced over to him and lifted a questioning eyebrow.

He shrugged. "I know. I don't know what gaffers do either. But that's where I'll be working."

They reached her family's private box as the orchestra was winding through its first movement. Bobby glanced back to her, his blue eyes sparkling with amusement. The private box was empty.

"Where's Auntie Loo?" she asked, expecting to find her aunt already here.

"She called and said she had a merger to oversee at the bank. It's just us tonight."

Soo-ling was shocked to find herself alone with Bobby—not that the two hadn't spent many long nights running the streets with each other. But this felt somehow different, both of them all dressed up and sharing this dark private space. She was grateful the lights were dimmed. It hid the warmth that bloomed in her cheeks.

Still, she hesitated outside the box seats, sensing something out of place. This was Auntie Loo's passion. Neither she nor Bobby were fans of the ballet. Plus a small part of her wanted to escape, to keep moving, troubled by an inexplicable sense of being trapped.

She rubbed her wrist and turned to Bobby. "You know, with Auntie Loo missing in action, we don't have to stay here. Over at the Grauman's, there's a movie retrospective of—"

"George Pal!" he finished. "I know! *War of the Worlds.* Those Sinbad movies."

She knew how much he loved special-effects film-making—from the old-fashioned miniature models and stop-motion photography of yesteryear to the newest computer-generated gadgetry. In many ways, he was just as trapped between the past and the present as she was, stuck between the traditional and the modern.

"Then let's go!" she said, catching his enthusiasm.

Laughing, they fled the ballet and escaped in the limo over to Hollywood Boulevard. They were the only patrons of the Grauman's Chinese Theatre that night decked out in a tuxedo and a formal silk gown. As they passed under the massive marquee, Bobby took her arm under his as if they were waltzing down the red carpet of a movie premiere.

Still, as much fun as it was, Soo-ling was all too conscious of the old theater's ancient Chinese symbolism and architecture. It stirred again the ghost of her mother.

But once they were seated, Bobby's enthusiasm sparked through her and pushed back any painful memories. He went on and on about why the director George Pal was the true father of the modern special effect, how stop-motion photography was a lost art. Then the houselights dimmed and the first movie started. A comfortable silence fell between them as they basked in the flickering glow that separated this world from the land of illusion.

At some point, her hand ended up in Bobby's. She could not say who took whose hand. It happened as naturally as the brush of a stroke of paint.

Still, neither dared look at the other, their gazes fixed toward the screen.

As the lights finally rose during the retrospective's intermission, she turned to Bobby, ready to fill the silence with empty words. She wasn't ready yet to discuss where their relationship would go from here. Her hand slipped from his.

"Bobby—"

Pain erupted in her chest, a whirling blast of ice and fire that burned away any words. Gasping, she fell toward the floor. The theater faded to black as she slipped into pure shadow.

As darkness drowned her, laughter accompanied her on the journey. The black amusement coalesced into a voice, hoary with frost. "Next time, my dear. Next time you are mine."

An image briefly flashed in her mind of the proprietor of the 7-Eleven. He lay faceup in a widening spiral of blood, a raw-edged wound gaping in his chest.

Then nothing, darkness again.

Reality snapped back into focus. Bobby's face filled her vision. She watched his lips move, but it took a moment for his words to make sense. "—hurt. Soo-ling, are you all right?"

She struggled to sit up. "Y-y-yes. I think so."

"Should I call a doctor? It looked like you fainted."

"No, Bobby. I just need to go home." The air in the theater seemed thinner, colder.

"I'll go with you."

She didn't have the energy to argue. Leaning on his shoulder, she allowed herself to be half-carried out of the theater and down to the limousine.

"We need to get her home," Bobby told Charles.

"Please," she whispered, collapsing into the leathered interior. "Can we pass by that 7-Eleven on the way?"

She had to know for sure.

Bobby climbed in next to her and shared a worried glance with Charles.

Soon they were speeding down the highway, the traffic mercifully thin. She stared out the window, her breathing shallow. She clenched the edge of her seat with white knuckles. As they exited onto Santa Monica Boulevard, the traffic snarled because of a mass of sirens and flashing lights. They were gathered in front of the 7-Eleven store. A traffic cop, illuminated by a flaming red flare, waved them forward. The limousine glided past the store as a paramedic pushed a draped gurney into a waiting ambulance.

"Do you wish to stop, miss?"

"No."

She'd seen what she needed to see.

"You tagged this store, didn't you?" Bobby asked, touching her hand, sensing her distress.

She nodded.

"But you couldn't finish your tag? Like back in Laguna?"

She remembered. It was early in her new role as protector of the city. She hadn't really fully believed it herself. She'd allowed the police to chase them off before she'd completed her mark. Afterward a fire burned down that store.

Even after that, she hadn't been truly convinced. Still wasn't. She had taken up the *fu* tag in memory of her mother, to honor her, a duty to tradition born out of guilt and loss.

But now this . . .

"No," she answered softly. "I finished it. It's something else." She remembered the icy claw and the black laughter. Words came tumbling out. She felt stupid even saying them, but she knew they were true. "I think something knows about me—and is hunting me."

Bobby remained silent. She knew he couldn't fully comprehend and probably didn't really believe in her powers, even though he had been the one to get her started. Bobby knew how deeply her mother's death had wounded her. One night, she had shared her mother's stories with him, her claims of a mystical maternal bloodline. Intrigued, Bobby had suggested using the symbol as her new tag, to add weight and purpose to their nightly runs together. And so it began.

But down deep—deeper than she cared to acknowledge—Soo-ling had always known it was more than that. She could not explain it. Tragedies drew her, called to her—and with a can of spray paint she could somehow prevent them.

Until now.

"What are you going to do?" Bobby finally asked.

"I don't know."

"Should I call Auntie Loo?"

Soo-ling frowned. Her mother's youngest sister, Auntie

Loo, had taken Soo-ling in after her mother had died. Her aunt was a loan officer for Bank of America, practical and serious. She pooh-poohed the ancient traditions her mother held so dear.

"I'm not sure Auntie Loo can help with this."

Or would even want to, for that matter.

But she might know something, anything to make sense of all of this. With no choice, Soo-ling fished out her iPhone. Her fingers trembled, making it hard to call up her aunt's number from the phone's contact list.

Bobby reached and covered her hand with his own. He squeezed once, then slipped the phone from her fingers. "Let me."

"Thanks."

She folded her hands in her lap to stop them from shaking. She stared out the window as Bobby called her aunt. His voice dissolved into the background hum of traffic.

She spent the drive home struggling to understand. Someone knew of her work. Or some*thing*—

Her sight suddenly glazed over, narrowing down into darkness. She blindly clawed for Bobby's hand. She clung to him as if she were drowning. But this time, she knew what was happening.

A vision opened inside her. She saw it all.

. . . *a sun rising over the ocean . . . a shoreline bucking and tearing . . . cliff-side homes crashing into the sea . . .*

Screams filled her ears.

Then a blank masonry wall appears . . . under the highway exit sign for Riverside . . . above a hidden fault line.

She knew what that meant. The blank wall was her next canvas. It called for her work . . . called for her protection against this coming tragedy. As the vision began to fade, she felt both relieved and terrified. Even after three years, these callings spooked her down to the marrow of her bones. She could no longer dismiss them as coincidences or nightmares born out of anxiety and guilt.

As the screams of the dying faded, mocking laughter followed.

She recognized that trail of dark amusement. It was the hunter revealing himself, letting his presence be known. It was both a challenge and a warning to her.

Bobby took her in his arms and held her to him. "What's wrong, Soo?"

She hid her face in her hands, not wanting Bobby to see her so distraught and scared. In a corner of her mind, she still heard the jeering laughter over the screams.

"An earthquake. Tomorrow," she finally mumbled into

his tuxedo jacket. "I can block it, but he'll try to stop me."

"Who?"

"I don't know, but we need to hurry. I need answers."

". . . only old stories." Auntie Loo paced the red Moroccan rug of the living room. Cigarette smoke traced her path. She was a stocky woman who cut her black hair into a fierce bob, nothing like the slender grace of Soo-ling's mother. "Mumbo jumbo nonsense. All incense and pseudoreligion."

"Auntie, I don't have time for this. You've been keeping secrets all my life." Soo-ling sat straighter on the leather couch next to Bobby. "Mother knew I had the power, and she must have told you."

"Soo-Ling, you don't truly believe—"

"Something is coming for me," she said, cutting her off. "I know it."

A cloud of fear passed over her aunt's features.

"It will tear this city apart to get to me," Soo-ling pressed.

Auntie Loo turned away to study the intricacies of a dynasty vase. Her voice became a faint whisper. "If you're right, then he's found you."

Soo-ling's heart skipped a beat. "Who?"

Her aunt refused to turn around, as if afraid to face any of this. It didn't fit into her world of spreadsheets and financial appraisals.

"Please, Auntie, *who*? Tell me."

"*Gui sou*," her aunt finally whispered, seeming to sag under the weight of ancient history. "The demon."

A stirring deep within Soo-ling responded to the quiet syllables: *gui sou*. With the beast named, her body knew it.

"What do you know, Auntie?"

"Just stories. Told to scare children to bed. Nothing but myths."

Soo-ling crossed the room to her aunt and hugged her from behind. Auntie Loo trembled in her embrace. "Not myths, Auntie. They're as real as my flesh."

Her aunt broke their embrace and crossed to the fireplace. "I did not want to believe."

"But why?"

"The family stories tell of dishonor. Cowardice and shame. Our family is a disgraced line. I was supposed to tell you when you came of age. But it seemed like fiction. I thought I could protect you from needless shame by concealing our family secret."

"But I don't understand. Having this power, this ability to protect, should be an honor."

Auntie tapped out her cigarette on a crystal ashtray. "It was. *Once.* Our clan was one of thirty-five chosen families, one from each province of China. Each family had the responsibility to protect its province. Our family guarded the Shandong Province on the coast of the Yellow Sea. We were a cherished clan in China."

"So what happened?" Bobby asked.

"As the story is told, the gods of order and chaos are always at war. Guardian families grew to be a part of this balance. They were gifted with the ability to interrupt certain strands of chaos and deflect disasters."

"Like I can do," Soo-ling said.

Auntie nodded and sat on the arm of a leather chair. "Yes. But over the passing centuries, the Chaos Lord became enraged at our interferences and forged a hunter from a part of his spleen, the *gui sou*, to destroy the guardian families. This hunter was unleashed, and many were destroyed before the families finally banded together. Each family sent one representative to form a union powerful enough to entrap the hunter. It took thirty-five guardians to encircle the beast and trap him, but before the enchantment was complete, one member—the one representing our family—panicked and fled. With the circle broken, the spell unraveled. The hunter destroyed the remaining thirty-four guardians. Our disgraced family was banished from China. After decades of wandering, we finally settled here."

"But what of the beast?"

"The story told is that the *gui sou* was injured by the failed assault and can only regain his full strength to push back into our world by finishing the destruction of the circle of guardians. He knows the power of the guardian is passed to only one member of each generation." Auntie Loo stared hard at her. "There is only one member left of that direct descendant line."

Soo-ling crossed back to the sofa and plopped down. "And of course that would be me."

Auntie Loo nodded.

Bobby took her hand, a silent promise that she was not alone.

"So how am I supposed to stop such a creature? It took thirty-five experienced guardians to stop him in the past. I am only one. Where am I going to find so many others before the sun rises?"

"I don't know. The stories give no other clue."

Soo-ling closed her eyes. If she did nothing, then L.A. was doomed. But how could she face this demon alone?

From the hallway, an ancient grandfather clock, an heirloom of three generations, chimed once. They were running out of night.

Bobby spoke up. "I have an idea. But it's a long shot."

Soo-ling turned to him doubtfully. "How?"

"Magic."

At two in the morning, the studio lot still bustled. Spot-lights and sodium lamps held back the night. Levi's-clad wranglers from a new Western mingled with black-robed ninjas from an action film, while prop men and camera crews scurried to and fro.

No one paid attention to Soo-ling and Bobby as they hurried across the lot.

"What if we're caught?" she asked, sticking close to his side.

Bobby pointed to his back. He'd replaced his tuxedo coat with a bomber jacket. The logo for Titan Pictures was stenciled on the back. "Got it with my internship. No one will give us a second glance."

She must have looked little convinced.

"No worries," he assured her. "This is the land of il-lusion. It's not about who you are—but who you *appear* to be."

He flipped up the collar of his jacket.

Soo-ling glanced around as they left the chaos and headed into a quieter section of the studio. Bobby had never fully explained his plan. "Where are we going?"

Her friend kept walking.

"Bobby . . ."

He stopped and faced her. "If that demon is tracking you, maybe we'd better keep this on a *need-to-know* basis. For now, the less you know the better."

For the first time, she read the fear in his face. He suddenly looked both older and younger at the same time. His eyes shone in the darkness, full of worry—but beneath that something more, something that had always been there, only she'd failed to recognize it. Until now.

"You don't have to do this," he said. "It's not too late. We could call both our families. Get the hell out of Dodge."

His words held their usual bounce, but she knew it was feigned, as much illusion as the rest of this place. He truly wanted her to flee, to run away, to live.

She acknowledged his fear—and what lay beneath it. Both gave her the strength to lean forward and tip up on her toes. *When had Bobby grown so tall?* She gently kissed his cheek, then lowered to her heels.

"I'm not going anywhere," she said firmly. "This is *our* city."

He smiled, blushing high in his cheeks. "Damn right it is."

Turning smartly on a heel, he led her away. And once

again, her hand somehow found its way into his. Together, they hurried through the maze of backlots and alleyways until he halted in front of a green door marked F/X.

"Special effects?" she asked, confused. "I don't understand."

Bobby finally relented. "Seems like we've reached that *need-to-know* moment."

As he explained his plan, her eyes grew huge. "Are you insane?" she gasped, and swatted him in the shoulder.

He rubbed his arm while shrugging. "If you have a better plan . . . ?"

She didn't—and they certainly didn't have time to come up with an alternative. She had to trust that Bobby knew what he was doing.

"Fine. Then let's do this."

His smile grew broader. "Who knew you were this easy?"

"Shut up."

Bobby used his studio keycard to unlock the door and enter the special-effects studio. She followed him up to a workroom on the second floor. It was full of computer equipment, giant plasma monitors, and a neighboring green-screen studio.

"Do you know how to run all this?"

Bobby gave her a how-stupid-do-I-look glare. "Who

grew up on Xbox and could hand-build his own computer from the age of nine? Besides, as an intern, I spent a few weeks here slinging coffee and doughnuts for the post-production crew. I learned everything I could. You'd be surprised what doors a Double Whip Mocha Latte will open for you here."

She turned in a circle. "What do I have to do?"

"First, you'll need a new outfit." He pointed to a row of black spandex suits hanging on a row of pegs. The bodysuits had Ping-Pong balls glued all over them. "You can change behind that curtain."

She took a deep breath, grabbed the smallest of the suits, and retreated behind the curtain. She quickly stripped to her bra and panties and shimmied into the tight outfit. Once done, she stared down at her body. The spandex clung like a second skin. She felt naked—and stupid.

White Ping-Pong balls marked each joint and curve of her body.

"What's taking you so long?" Bobby called to her. "I'm all set here."

She stepped from behind the curtain and pointed to him. "Not a word!"

His mouth dropped open at the sight of her. He lifted

a finger to his chin and closed his mouth, but his grin remained and spoke volumes.

He crossed to her and handed her a pair of goggles that looked like a large black scuba mask. The goggles trailed a set of black cords.

"What now?" she asked.

He pointed to the neighboring studio, wrapped all in green. "The motion-capture suit works best against a green screen. Put on the goggles and you'll see everything I do on the computer."

Bobby walked her into the empty studio and helped her put on the heavy goggles. The inside of the mask was one big digital screen. A computerized test pattern filled her vision.

"Okay," he said. "Just stand there until I say go."

"Then what?"

"Do what you do best. I'll run the controls while you just paint."

She heard him plug in the goggle's cords, then retreat out of the studio. The door closed. She felt suddenly alone. Over the years she had developed a suspicion of technology, going back to the machines that had failed to keep her mother alive. She had turned instead to what her mother loved: the simplicity of oil on canvas, of spray paint on walls. That was magic enough for her. She had no use for the cold calculating world of computer technology.

That was Bobby's domain.

She had to trust him—did trust him.

Bobby's voice reached her through tiny speakers built into the goggles. "Soo, wave your arms for me. I want to make sure the computer is properly capturing your motion."

She obeyed, feeling silly.

"That's it! Perfect calibration. I'm activating you now."

The test pattern in her goggles dissolved away, and she found herself staring into a new world. It appeared as if she were standing in front of an easel in the middle of a meadow brimming with wildflowers. Butterflies fluttered among the blossoms while birds spun and twittered. She raised an arm to block out the sunlight—only it wasn't her arm that rose in front of her, but a computer-generated facsimile.

"Is it too bright?" Bobby's voice whispered from tiny speakers in the goggles. "It's hard to judge from the monitor."

"Yes . . . a little too much glare."

"I'll adjust."

Soo-ling squinted into the meadow. The sun suddenly sank toward the horizon, shadows stretching.

"How's that?" he asked.

"Much better," she said. "But what do I do now?"

"Paint your tag, Soo. That attracted the beast before. Call him into the virtual world. I'll record from here."

Steeling herself, she inhaled sharply and reached for the paintbrush and palette of oils. Though nothing was truly in front of her, the motion and response was so perfect that it made her feel like it was. She swore she could almost feel the brush in one hand and the palette in the other.

After a few fumbling attempts, she fell into her usual rhythm. She dabbed her brush into the oil and tentatively drew her first stroke, a slash of crimson on the white canvas. The remaining thirteen strokes completed her characteristic tag in a few breaths.

Clutching her virtual paintbrush, she waited.

Nothing happened.

"Bobby?"

"Did you paint it correctly, Soo?"

She studied her work. It was perfect.

What am I forgetting?

Then it dawned on her. She reached a finger through

empty air, while in another world, a computer-generated finger rose and reached for the center of the painted glyph on the canvas. As contact was made, a familiar tingling surged up her arm. Soo-ling tensed, holding her breath. She waited for several heartbeats.

Still nothing.

She started to drop her arm when a stabbing cold seized her wrist. She wanted desperately to pull away like before—but she knew this time she must stand firm, hold fast, not disgrace the family as her ancestor had done so many centuries ago.

Foreign memories suddenly flooded into her consciousness, like dreams long forgotten slipping back into focus again. She remembered Shandong Province with the sun rising over the Yellow Sea; she remembered fishing with her brothers, cherry blossoms floating on the water; she remembered her first love, Wan Lee, turning his back on her after her shame.

"Soo?" Bobby had an uncertain edge to his voice. "What are you doing? There's this old woman dressed in a robe on the screen where you're supposed to be."

Soo-ling barely heard him, floating between past and present. She began to understand as more ancestral memories filled her.

"She's a friend," she finally mumbled, knowing it to be true. "I don't know quite what's happening, but your hunch was right. It's coming. I sense it. Like electricity before a thunderstorm."

The cold crept up her arm, seeking her heart. Dusty laughter, old and cracked, followed and crumbled into words. "I have found you at long last, *siu far*, my little flower."

Distant memories intruded. A foggy glen, surrounded by towering trees, the lowing of cattle from a distant rice paddy, and a creature of nightmares crouching, its voice mocking.

Soo-ling's lips moved, but she did not know who spoke: herself or her ancestor. "*Gui sou.*"

More dark laughter. "Ah, you know my name. You have hidden well over the years, *siu far*. But now it is time to be plucked. I shall wear you as an ornament once I am free. Free to stalk the world of man."

A mist rose from the meadow floor and coalesced into an ancient face, yellow and wrinkled like a dried apricot. The face split into a leer, lined by fangs. The fog continued to encircle her, forming the coils of a snake—along with a reptilian claw that gripped her wrist.

Old fears arose, like smoke from an extinguished fire.

Trapped, must escape, flee!

Her head throbbed, and the world began to tilt, eyes blurring.

"Soo-ling!" Bobby's voice jolted her to the present. "I can see that monster on the monitor. Get out of there!"

The spiked and scaled body of the beast appeared in the mist. She began to yank her arm away when a foreign thought intruded.

No. Stand firm, child. You must resist.

"Soo, I'm ending the program."

"No, Bobby!" she yelled. Understanding dawned in her. "The circle isn't complete. It will follow me out."

"Let it try!" Bobby said. "I'll take care of it."

His words—full of bravura and love—conjured more recent memories. *Running the back alleys with Bobby. Fleeing police and gang members, laughing. Planting tags throughout the city. My city! Our city!*

"Just do as we planned," she said. "Complete the circle."

The *gui sou* leaned closer, suspicious, its breath stale as an open grave. "Who do you speak to, little one? Prayers, perhaps? Do not bother seeking aid from your puny gods. Prayers will not save you."

"Who needs prayers, when you've got friends who love you?" And she knew it to be true. "Now, Bobby!"

"Engaging copies!"

The empty meadow suddenly filled with thirty-four other easels, exact copies of her original. They encircled the field. Disembodied arms, floating free, repeated what she had painted earlier. Thirty-four arms picked up brushes and palettes and painted identical symbols in unison. Then they all reached forward to touch the center of their glyphs.

A flash of confusion swept over the creature's jaundiced features. Its fiery eyes darted everywhere. The claws gripping her hand faded back to mist. Snaking coils dissolved back to fog. The mocking face leaned close. "What trick is this, witch?"

She knew the answer. "A spell broken long ago is woven again."

"Impossible. There are no other guardians. What trickery is this?"

The *gui sou* collected its mists, like a woman gathering her skirts, and glided across the meadow. It tried to break out of the circle but was stopped by an invisible wall of force. It flattened its mists against the barrier, probing for an opening. With a shriek, it thrashed back and forth across the meadow, flinging itself against the sides of its new prison.

After a full minute, it stopped and rushed at her. "Drop your arm, *siu far*, break the circle, and I will let you escape again."

Same old trick.

"Not this century," she sneered.

"You'll never be able to stand there forever," it warned, rearing up in threat and fury. "You'll tire! Then I will devour you!"

She faced the monster with an arched eyebrow. "Really? Then let me welcome you to the new millennium! You're nothing but a ghost of the past. And the past is where you will remain. Locked forever in *memory*." She called more loudly. "Bobby, *hit it!*"

"Saving to disk now!"

The world within the goggles pulled away, shrinking smaller and smaller until the digital window was the size of a postage stamp. As it receded, she saw them appear, standing behind each of the other easels: different Chinese women, of varying ages, the murdered provincial guardians from the ancient past. They bowed to her, acknowledging an ancient debt paid in full.

At the last moment, a whisper reached her, full of love and pride.

Si low chai . . .

She knew that voice, those tender words. Tears welled, bursting from her swollen heart.

". . . Mother . . ."

A warmth filled her as the tenuous connection faded.

Soo-ling struggled to hold it—but it was like grasping smoke. The connection ended, as it must. That was not her world.

Still, the warmth remained inside her.

The true ghost of her mother.

Her everlasting love.

The image of a computer desktop snapped into place inside her goggles. It held frozen the last picture: thirty-five guardians encircling a demon. Then that file dropped away into a computerized folder icon. A symbol of a combination lock overlay the folder. It *clicked* closed.

"We're locked up!" Bobby called out.

Soo-ling took a long, shuddering breath, then pulled off her goggles. She stood again in the empty studio. Behind her, the door banged open and Bobby rushed inside. His expression grew concerned as he saw her face.

"Soo, are you all right?"

She wiped her tears. "Never better."

And she meant it.

Bobby crossed to her and handed her a recordable

DVD. A thin crust of frost caked its surface. "It should be trapped in there, right?"

She nodded and took the DVD. "I hope so."

"So then we've won," Bobby said, blowing out his relief.

"The battle, perhaps, but not the war."

She knew the *gui sou* was only a small part of the Chaos Lord. There was still a wall in Riverside that needed her handiwork—or come dawn, Los Angeles would really rock and roll.

Bobby stood before her. "What now?"

"Time to go to work. Do you have a can of spray paint?"

He raised his eyebrows as if insulted. "Of course."

She leaned and tipped up on her toes again. This time she kissed his lips. "Then let's go save the world."

RAY GUN

· TIM MALEENY ·

When you're sixteen you often dream of being a hero, but rarely do you actually get to save the world. Ray just hoped he was up for the task.

His full name was Raymond Gunstein but friends called him Ray, and his dad called him Ray Gun, which he kind of liked. If he really were a hero—a superhero, with a badass costume and everything—that's what he'd want to be called. But right at this moment, hanging from the roof of a speeding train, he had bigger problems than choosing a nickname.

Ray tightened his grip and watched as blood ran down

his leg, over his ankle, then vanished in the rushing wind. The train was moving at over a hundred miles an hour, so no matter how much he bled, not a single drop would hit the tracks below. And if he lost his grip, they could scrape a mile of track and still not find enough DNA to identify the body.

It was a new high-speed rail, much faster than the Amtrak commuter train that used to run from New York to Washington. Each car had a door at both ends. Signs all over the train advised passengers to hold on carefully when moving between cars, and a white placard with red letters warned that climbing ladders to the roof of the train was *strictly prohibited* while the train was in motion, even for railroad employees. Ray's mom was a lawyer, so he knew what *prohibited* meant—it meant only an idiot would climb onto the roof of a speeding train.

I must be an idiot, thought Ray, hanging on to the narrow railing that ran along the roof of the dining car. Ray took a deep breath and tensed his muscles, hoping he had enough strength to climb to the top of the train.

It all started with a lost lizard.

Ray had been sitting in his compartment across from his dad. They'd left the door open so it wouldn't feel too cramped, and the corridor was empty. Not that Ray's dad would have noticed, his head barely visible above the screen of his laptop.

"That's bad for your eyes, Dad."

"Mm-hmm." Ray's dad was named Phil, and he was a scientist, which apparently involved being absent-minded. So Ray already knew what his dad was going to say. "Forgot my reading glasses. Bet they're on my desk at home."

Ray yawned and took out his iPhone. "Want to play chess?"

Phil Gunstein looked up from the screen and smiled. "I'd love to—*later*—but right now I have to run some numbers."

Ray was on spring break, traveling with his dad to a scientific conference in D.C. His mom was back in New York, preparing for an important case coming to trial. Something to do with a big energy company, accusations of fraud, and a senator who just got indicted. Unlike a lot of his friends, Ray got along well with his parents, but these days it seemed like they were married to their work instead of to each other.

His dad squinted at the screen. "It looks like the phase induction is a lot bigger than I projected. Could be a problem."

At any given time, Ray liked to think he understood

about half of what his dad was talking about. This wasn't one of those times.

"Does your, um, phasing problem have anything to do with your presentation at the conference?" Ray thought he sounded less clueless than he felt.

His dad scratched his head with both hands, a sign he was struggling to make a complicated idea sound simple. "You know all the buzz about alternative fuels?"

Ray nodded. His school had been on a green crusade for some time. Recycling, composting, homework sent by e-mail to save paper. "Wind power, solar. Renewable energy."

"Solar, sure . . . or something entirely new." His dad raised his eyebrows dramatically. "Think *Starship Enterprise*."

"Antimatter?" Ray leaned forward. His dad had DVD box sets for every season of *Star Trek* and *The Next Generation;* the entire family had been hooked since Ray was a kid. "You're not serious."

His dad nodded. "That's why I've spent so much time at CERN."

Thanks to Google, Ray had seen countless pictures of CERN, so although he'd never been there, he visualized the underground complex as soon as his dad said the name. The home of the world's largest particle accelerator, built at the border of Switzerland and France. A race-track ten miles in diameter, powered by electromagnets, where physicists sent subatomic particles racing close to the speed of light, smashing them together to see what might happen. CERN was a demolition derby for atoms.

"We discovered a simple way to create antimatter." Phil Gunstein frowned. "But some people aren't happy about it."

"Like?"

"Some of the energy companies still heavily vested in oil, or those who want to control the discovery for themselves. And a few skeptics who think we might accidentally create a black hole that would eat the planet." He said "black hole" nonchalantly, as if discussing the weather, but the idea grabbed Ray's imagination in a choke hold.

"Will you?" Ray visualized a black ball with red eyes and sharp teeth gnawing its way through the planet like a worm through an apple.

"Not a chance." Phil Gunstein looked suddenly impatient, like he'd been forced to defend his theories for too long. "That's just a dumb idea started by people who never studied science. Unfortunately most politicians fall into that category. That's why we're holding this press conference, to share our discovery with the world."

Ray already knew who his dad meant by *we*—the four

other physicists on his team, two men and two women, meeting them in Washington later that day.

"See for yourself." Phil winked, then rummaged around a small suitcase until he found a metal canister. It looked like a stainless-steel thermos. There was a clear band running around the middle of the container, a translucent window into the device. Holding the object tightly at either end, Phil Gunstein twisted his hands in opposing directions and said, "Let there be light."

Ray felt the hairs on his arm stand up and suddenly the cabin filled with a brilliant blue-green light. The center of the canister was glowing like a miniature sun.

Ray looked away until his dad twisted the two ends back to their original position. A tickling sensation ran down his spine, then everything returned to normal. Ray tried to blink away the spots in his eyes.

"Cool." He didn't know what else to say. And he did think his dad's work was cool, even though he sometimes wished his dad would get as excited about his life as he did about his life's work.

"Thought you'd get a kick out of that." His dad held the thermos like a trophy. "The antimatter in this container could power an electric car for ten years."

"And it's safe?" Ray trusted his dad implicitly, but the image of a hungry black hole had made an impression.

"Perfectly safe—unless you believe in *string theory*, but most physicists have moved on." His dad looked almost embarrassed. "The stuff of science fiction, not science fact."

"Tell me."

His dad made a dismissive gesture but kept talking. Ray knew once you got Phil Gunstein talking about his work, the real trick was getting him to shut up. "Some people think there are other dimensions, other worlds." He spread the fingers of his right hand and waved them in front of Ray's eyes. "Places where people like us might be moving around, right here, in the spaces in between things." He closed his fingers into a fist, one by one. "Harness this kind of energy, then *theoretically* you could open a doorway."

"And the people *there* could reach over *here*?" Ray shifted in his seat and pocketed the iPhone, neglected on his lap. This was getting interesting.

"Nobody knows." His dad made a face. "That's one of the problems with string theory. Some think only energy could pass through, but if matter and energy are the same, why not something solid? It would be like moving from two dimensions to three, or from three to four— why not five or six? But even fringe scientists admit no living creature could survive the journey. . . ." His voice trailed off as he shook his head at his own foolishness.

"But what if something could come across?"

"Some*thing*, as opposed to someone?"

"Maybe a weapon." Ray shrugged. "Or psychic energy. Or a message . . ."

"Maybe aliens?" His dad smiled. "You've been reading too many comic books."

"They're graphic novels," said Ray, his turn to sound impatient.

That's when they heard the scream.

It was a high-pitched yell followed by a curse, which preceded a blur that transformed into a girl. A girl in a hurry. She dashed into the corridor as Ray jumped to his feet and almost slammed into her.

"Have you seen my gecko?" The girl didn't miss a beat, just looked frantically past Ray, down at the floor, searching. She was Ray's age, give or take, with reddish hair and eyes that looked brown under the fluorescent lights. She was cute—more than cute, actually. She waved a hand in front of his eyes, then snapped her fingers, and Ray realized he was staring. "A gecko . . . *hello?*"

"Sorry, no." Ray shrugged apologetically.

"It's a lizard, a little green lizard," said the girl. "Name's Greeny."

Ray held out his hand. "Ray."

"My *gecko's* name is Greeny." She smiled and took a breath, as if really noticing Ray for the first time. "*My* name is Amanda." Her eyes radiated warmth as they locked on his face. When she blinked the connection was broken and Ray felt a pang of regret. His last girlfriend was a distant memory.

"Sorry about your lizard."

"Not your fault." Amanda looked back toward the neighboring compartment. "I'm traveling with my aunt—Aunt *Edith*—and she . . ." Amanda took a step closer and lowered her voice. " . . . has a *dog*." She made it sound like her aunt's dog ownership was a source of great embarrassment.

"I always wanted a dog," said Ray, loud enough for his dad to hear, though it wouldn't be the first time he'd heard it.

"This isn't a real dog," said Amanda dismissively. "It's alive, of course, but it's a *lap*dog. One of those yappy little things. Do you know why lapdogs were bred, back in Europe during the late 1600s?"

Ray shook his head.

"To attract fleas." Amanda nodded. "It's true. People didn't have running water, and they didn't bathe much." She wrinkled her nose. "So the idea was that if you had a lapdog, the fleas would jump *off* you"—she reached forward and pressed a finger against Ray's chest—"and *onto* your dog."

"Did it work?"

"Got me." Amanda shrugged. "But that dog is a menace."

"How come?"

"Because lizards are afraid of dogs!" Amanda puffed out her cheeks. "Guess I should have thought of that before letting Greeny out of his box." She scanned the corridor again. "I think he ran toward the dining car."

"Let's go look."

"Aren't you the gentleman." Amanda gave Ray an appraising glance. He felt himself starting to blush, so he looked over his shoulder. "Dad, I'm going for a walk." His dad waved absently, his head already hidden behind his laptop.

The train rocked back and forth as they moved toward the next car. Ray scanned the carpet but the light in the corridor was dim. The doors to the other compartments were all closed. No geckos.

They came to the end of the car, a sliding door with a round window.

"You been in there?" Amanda jutted her chin toward the door.

Ray shook his head. "Not yet."

"Dining car." Amanda smacked her lips. "Let's go."

"What about Greeny?"

Amanda looked down at the floor, along the walls, up at the ceiling. "He's run away before but always comes back." She sighed. "Truth is, I usually don't find him until he finds me."

With a hard pull, she yanked open the sliding door. Fresh air and train noises washed over them. Instead of the *clack-clack-clack* of older trains, the wheels hummed, almost at a subsonic level. Ray could feel the vibrations through the soles of his shoes.

Carefully they stepped between cars. With another pull, they found themselves in the dining car. Ray heard a rumbling and realized it was his stomach. His dad always forgot to eat once absorbed in his work, and Ray had lost track of time. Lunch had come and gone, but the dining car never closed. Along the right side of the car, small tables were covered with cold cuts, bread, condiments. Enough food to stop a famine.

"This is sick," said Ray, building himself a sandwich.

"*Nuh-hmm-umm-huh?*" Amanda smiled broadly, her mouth already full. She had moved left, where a long table covered by a white tablecloth held the desserts.

Chocolate balls stacked in pyramids like cannonballs on a pirate ship. A chocolate cake carved into triangle slices, the whole thing bigger than a large pizza. Enough cookies to crush a whole troop of Girl Scouts.

"Sorry?"

Amanda swallowed whatever she was eating in one huge gulp. "I said 'Not bad, huh?'"

Ray smiled and looked across the tables. "Not bad at all." The afternoon train was half-empty, most commuters preferring the morning express, so they had the car to themselves. But ten minutes later Ray had to get out of there. His stomach was bulging and an ache was on its way. An all-you-can-eat buffet and a sixteen-year-old male was a dangerous combination under any circumstances.

Amanda nodded her agreement when he said, "Let's go find your lizard."

Dizzy from the sugar rush, they lurched across the connecting platform into their car and almost collided with a man standing just on the other side of the sliding door.

"Oops." Amanda was first through the door. "Excuse me."

The man said nothing. He was tall, much taller than Ray, and his skin had an unhealthy pallor. He wore a baggy suit, white shirt, and gray tie, and in his right hand he held a stainless-steel briefcase. His eyes were concealed by a pair of mirrored sunglasses.

Ray could see his own reflection in the lenses. He started to step aside to let the man pass, but for the second time that day, Amanda's scream locked his feet to the floor.

In the confined space the noise startled both Ray and the stranger, who stumbled backward and dropped his briefcase. Ray instinctively bent down and grabbed it, ready to apologize, thinking *Amanda must have seen her gecko, that's why she screamed.* But as he leaned forward, Ray caught her expression and looked more closely at the man in the sunglasses.

"Amanda," he said in a voice he didn't recognize as his own. "Run . . . *now!*"

The sunglasses now sat askew on the man's face, exposing one eye. An eye unlike any Ray had ever seen. Deep yellow, with a vertical slit for a pupil. The kind of eye you'd find on a cat or a snake, not a human being. The stranger blinked, and an eyelid the color of sour milk slid sideways.

Then he reached for his briefcase.

Ray gazed at the man's hand, the skin of his forearm

as the jacket pulled back. Skin that had looked jaundiced in the weak light was, up close, really a dull green. This wasn't a man at all.

Amanda was on the balls of her feet, standing to the man's left. Ray was on the right, still holding the briefcase. He couldn't chase them both.

Ray made a decision. Taking a step backward, he pulled open the door that separated the cars.

From the corner of his eye Ray sensed the man reaching, a peripheral vision of a moss-colored hand and yellow eye, but Ray was already gone, leaping across the platform into the dining car. He sprinted the length of the car and didn't look over his shoulder until he reached the far end.

The good news was the stranger hadn't chased Amanda. The bad news was that he was chasing Ray.

Chasing wasn't exactly the right word, because the man walked as if he had all the time in the world. His movements were deliberate, the legs stiff, his knees not bending the way they should. Step by painful step he advanced, as inexorable as the tide. As relentless as the monsters that hide under your bed.

The sunglasses were back in place, and for an instant Ray tried to convince himself it had all been his imagination. A full stomach, a pretty girl, a trick of the light. But any hopes were shattered when the man opened his mouth and his face tore itself in half.

The jaw wasn't hinged like a human mouth but was set farther back, so the top half of his head swung open like the tailgate of a truck, exposing row upon row of conical teeth. They glinted in the diffuse light of the car, each a white spear dripping with saliva. Ray didn't need a written invitation. He turned around and yanked the door handle with all his strength and lurched forward.

Only to smash his face against the glass. The door was locked.

Ray jerked the handle again, peered across the platform at the next car. *Where is the conductor?* He banged on the window but nearly broke his hand, his fist making a dull *thud* against the thick glass. *Did the creature come from this side of the train and then lock the door? Is there anyone in the next compartment, or are they all dead?* Either way, Ray was trapped. He felt the blood drain from his face as he turned to his captor, wondering if the man would be standing right behind him.

The man wasn't standing at all. In the brief time Ray had turned his back, the *creature*—Ray couldn't think of a better word for it—had clearly decided it would be easier to climb the walls than learn how to walk on two feet. It still came slowly but its movements were more confident. Fingers spread, it moved along the wall like a spider, legs splayed as it crawled forward.

Ray considered dropping the briefcase, making a mad dash for the exit, but the car was too narrow. He was stuck unless the creature decided to let him go.

Yeah, right.

Ray scanned the long tables, searching for something he could use as a weapon. Plastic forks and knives, white bread and cold cuts. Chocolate balls. Not a steak knife in sight. His gaze shifted to the windows, where a frantic blur of trees and telephone poles passed by.

The windows!

The creature flexed its jaw as it crept closer, exposing a forked tongue that squirmed like an angry worm.

Ray started moving before a plan even formed in his mind. He took off his belt. Quickly he looped it through the handle of the briefcase, then slung it over his shoulder, wearing the case like a messenger bag. And before the creature closed the gap between them another foot, Ray was opening the nearest window.

The rush of air almost knocked him backward, and it took all his strength to lean outside. He held his breath and pushed, squeezing his upper body through the top half of the window, twisting as he dragged the bag behind him. A small ledge ran across the top of the window to deflect rain or any debris, and Ray could just reach it if he stretched.

His eyes started to water, and the reflection off the glass made it almost impossible to see clearly into the car. But Ray knew he didn't have much time. He pulled his left leg outside and pressed it against the window ledge.

Then he felt a damp cold wrap itself around his right ankle and almost lost his grip. As he pressed his face against the window, his worst fear was confirmed. The creature's jaw had unhinged, the forked tongue tickling Ray's calf as the head slid forward. Its rubbery hand was holding his right leg like a drumstick.

Ray gripped the railing in both hands and twisted sideways, swinging his left foot through the open window and catching the creature on the chin. The jaw snapped back, bottom teeth tearing across Ray's calf like broken glass. A searing pain followed by a release of pressure as the creature loosened its grip.

Palms sweating, Ray kicked frantically against the side of the train, trying to boost himself up. His right leg was on fire, a river of blood soaking through his pants.

The rushing air was blinding. Now that they were

away from the city, the train seemed to be moving even faster. The track below was an angry blur. Ray thought he might pass out.

Pull! He got an elbow over the railing but slipped. Ray cried out as his body floated away from the train, gravity failing, until he realized they must have hit a turn. He adjusted his grip, one hand at a time, and tried to swing his legs sideways.

That's when he saw a green hand claw its way through the window. It swept to the right, searching blindly. Ray gritted his teeth and swung to the left.

His leg hooked the railing and he rolled onto the roof of the train, facing back the way he had come, toward his compartment and his dad. But it was a long car. Hand locked around the railing, he slowly inched his way forward across the roof, wiggling back and forth on his belly, his face grazing the roof of the train. He felt the cool metal against his forehead and fought the urge to stop and close his eyes.

Ray was almost at the front of the car, near the ladder. Just another three feet. He could feel the weight of the briefcase, the strap biting into his shoulder. He felt weak and wasn't sure he could climb the ladder between the cars. He took a deep breath and risked a glance backward, his eyes following the red trail of his own blood.

The creature was following the same trail from the other direction.

The wind didn't seem to bother it. It lay perfectly still, eyes unfocused until the impossible tongue emerged between stalagmites of teeth to sample Ray's blood. Then its head pivoted toward Ray as the yellow eyes narrowed. It might be nearsighted, but it had found the scent.

C'mon, Ray, you can do this. Ray tore his gaze away from the creature and—

—*gasped.* They had rounded a bend, and straight ahead was the gaping mouth of a tunnel. The front of the train had already disappeared inside. Ray didn't know how much clearance there was between the train and the ceiling of the tunnel but it wasn't much. He only had seconds left.

You have to do this.

Ray lurched sideways and spun so his legs dangled between the cars. His right foot found the ladder first, and he grimaced at the pain. Fingers numb, one rung at a time till he hit the platform, hard.

Blackness.

There was a heavy *thunk* overhead, followed by a rolling, tumbling sound. Then the roar of the tunnel filled Ray's ears until he was deaf.

Heart beating like a jackhammer, Ray groped in the

darkness until he found the door handle and pulled with all the strength he had left.

"Lock that door!"

Ray's father caught him as he fell across the threshold. The conductor stepped forward and turned a key into a square hole at the side of the metal door, then tested the handle.

"Nobody's coming through there." The conductor was a stout man with a walrus mustache, and he looked angry. "I don't know *what* is going on with this train, but I intend to find out. Some businessman in first class claims somebody stole one of his suits, and the woman in the compartment next to him says her briefcase is missing. And now you folks claim—my God, son, what happened to your leg?"

"He fell." Ray's dad answered for him, his face grim.

Ray held on to his dad like a drowning sailor and kept his mouth shut. The conductor stalked over to the bathroom and emerged a moment later with a first-aid kit.

"Give me that." Ray's dad took the red-and-white box and half-carried his son back to the bathroom, where he expertly cleaned the wound. It hurt but wasn't as deep as Ray had feared, just a series of ugly furrows carved across the back of his leg. He'd done worse on a mountain bike. Once his dad had wrapped the cuts tightly in gauze, Ray saw a red pattern emerge but then slow and finally stop. No blood was soaking through. He'd have a scar—several, in fact—but he wasn't going to bleed to death.

The conductor poked his head through the door. "I'd suggest you folks lock yourselves in your compartments till I return—I'm going to check on the other passengers. And remember, there's an emergency call button in every car."

Ray let his dad gently nudge him along the corridor. Amanda emerged from her compartment, smiling bravely, then ran forward and gave Ray a hug. His hands started shaking from the adrenaline crash. Ray's dad gave his son another squeeze and helped him sit. Then he lifted the belt from around Ray's shoulders and said, "This a souvenir from your adventure?"

Ray nodded.

"Okay then, let's take a look inside that briefcase."

Amanda and Ray sat next to each other, across from his dad. Unconsciously she rested a hand on Ray's thigh, as if the danger had drawn them closer. He felt light-headed and wondered if it was just the loss of blood.

His dad popped the latches on the metallic case. The inside was empty of the usual things a briefcase would hold—no papers, pens, or folders—just five identical objects. They looked like crystals, long and narrow with angular surfaces. And trapped within each was a viscous solution, a green liquid that almost glowed.

"What are they?" asked Ray.

His dad didn't answer. Instead he picked up the first crystalline vial and held it close to his face. They were still inside the tunnel, so their window was a gray-black blur, the only light coming from a single bulb set into the ceiling.

Phil Gunstein almost dropped the object. Taking a deep breath, he steadied his grip and set the vial back inside the briefcase. He had a grave look on his face.

"Dad, what is it?"

His dad picked up the other vials and examined them one by one. Ray noticed for the first time that the bottom of each narrowed to a point, like a syringe.

"See for yourselves." Ray's dad lifted the first crystal vial so they could see the reflections moving across its surface.

Ray gasped. Inside the crystal was a perfect hologram of his father.

Every detail of his face, right down to the crow's-feet

around his eyes. He raised the next one and Ray recognized the face immediately—one of the women working with his father on the antimatter project.

Five vials for five scientists. Each with a perfect image of the recipient. His father had been first in line.

"What does it mean?" asked Amanda.

"I think these vials were meant to—"

"Kill you?" Ray blurted his worst fear.

His dad squinted at the vials. "Or make us forget." He looked at his son and forced a smile. "But thanks to you—*Ray Gun*—they failed." He paused and then added. "Whoever or whatever *they* are."

"But won't they—*it*—try again?"

His dad shook his head. "I don't think so—once we hold our press conference, they'll have no reason to come after the scientists." He paused, drew a breath. "I guess anything is possible—we opened a doorway by accident. They saw it first and slipped some*thing* into our world." He shrugged. "Maybe they're afraid of us."

"Afraid of *us*?" said Ray.

"Maybe they're afraid of what we'll do if we visit *their* world. After all, we haven't always done the best job with ours."

Ray visualized the creature on top of the train. It hadn't looked like it was afraid of anything.

"But if we opened the door," his dad continued, "we can keep it closed."

Ray looked up. "But that means abandoning your life's work."

"I won't give up, just change direction." His dad forced a smile. "Besides, I'm *looking* at my life's work." He placed a hand on Ray's shoulder.

Ray felt himself blush. He turned toward Amanda to see if she'd noticed.

"Ray Gun?" she said. "You're not serious."

Ray started to reply but was blinded by a burst of sunshine as they emerged from the tunnel. Everyone blinked and glanced outside. Ray could see rolling fields with horses and cows, speeding past like an out-of-control carousel. Amanda opened her mouth to make another remark, but Ray never heard her, because her voice was drowned out by a thousand pieces of glass exploding into the car.

The creature was still alive, and it was climbing through the broken window.

It moved like a folding chair, knees bending in the wrong direction as they extended through the window frame.

Ray's dad pulled them back toward the door. They could run to the next car, but they couldn't all climb onto the roof like Ray did, and he was too weak to try it again. The thing in the window wasn't going to stop.

His dad stared in disbelief but had enough presence of mind to push Ray closer to Amanda. Their eyes met, and Ray noticed for the first time that her eyes weren't brown at all but were dark green.

Green like a gecko. That's when he got the idea, and Ray knew from her expression Amanda was already there with him. She held his gaze for another second before dashing to the next compartment.

Amanda returned carrying a large plastic box with a wire mesh door. Ray could see a white furry ball with a wrinkled face, watery brown eyes. Amanda gingerly opened the door and made kissing sounds as she produced the smallest dog Ray had ever seen.

Amanda shielded the dog's eyes as she stepped across the compartment. Ray's dad was trying to position himself to shove the creature at just the right moment, but Ray knew the creature would be too strong. It had survived the tunnel, and a kick to the jaw had barely registered. It might not be graceful, but it was powerful.

Ray figured they had less than five seconds before the creature got far enough inside that it would be impossible to force it out again. He started counting in his head.

One. Ray's dad reached into his bag and produced

his antimatter gadget. "Maybe this will scare it," he said through gritted teeth. "Stand back."

Two. Amanda ignored him and squeezed in close to the window. She still had her hand over the dog's eyes, but the wind blew fiercely into the cabin, and the dog was growling deep in its throat.

Three. The creature's face became visible as it slid down from the roof. Its yellow eyes were glaring at them.

Four. Ray's dad started to twist the two halves of the stainless-steel container.

Five. Amanda thrust the terrified dog through the open window.

Amanda held on tightly as the dog barked furiously, clawing Amanda's arms in a frantic scramble to get back inside. She winced from the pain but didn't let go.

Ray watched as the creature's slit pupils narrowed in fear. Then a green light exploded in the cabin and Ray couldn't see anything at all.

Ray blinked the spots from his eyes and saw his dad leaning out the window.

When he was satisfied the creature was gone, Phil Gunstein pulled his head inside and dropped the metal canister onto the table. "I thought I'd try to blind it." He nodded at Amanda. "But I think your dog scared it silly." He petted the dog, which was still trembling.

Ray noticed deep scratches across Amanda's arms. "You okay?"

Amanda nodded as she left the cabin. Moments later she came back with a towel wrapped around her arms but without the dog. Ray reached for the first-aid kit but Amanda suddenly pushed past him and dropped to her knees.

"Greeny!"

Amanda laughed as a tiny lizard ran up her left arm and over her head, hiding itself in her red hair. She giggled and plucked it free, stood up, then held it by the tail only inches from her nose.

"No more running away, you hear me?" She looked at Ray. "Told you he'd find me." Greeny swung back and forth, upside down. Ray smiled until the tiny creature swiveled its head in his direction.

The lizard blinked, and Ray gasped as he made eye contact with the gecko.

He recognized those eyes. They had tracked him across the dining car, followed him across the roof of the train. He looked from the lizard to Amanda, who was staring at him once again as if she'd read his mind.

Ray felt the hairs on the back of his neck stand up and wondered if it was only a side effect of his father's invention. He blinked, but where he saw spots only moments before, now he saw only coincidences.

Ray glanced over at his dad, who was watching him and Amanda with a bemused expression, trying to connect the dots. Amanda still held the gecko only inches from his face. Ray forced a smile and said the first thing that came to mind.

"Hey, Dad, can we get a dog?"

Phil Gunstein looked from his son to the lizard, then back again.

"Ray Gun," he said, "I think that's a great idea."

ABOUT
THE AUTHORS

▾ R.L. STINE ▾

R.L. Stine loved horror stories as a kid, and when he discovered that the local barbershop carried copies of two horror comic books, he started getting a haircut every Saturday. He wrote lots of jokes and stories, kept writing through college, then moved to New York City to work as a writer. The first job he found was with a fan magazine, and he said that it was good training because it taught him to write fast and make up stuff.

He edited a humor magazine for a few years, but when it folded, he decided to try horror, and his series for teenagers, Fear Street, became a huge success. So he wrote a series for younger kids, Goosebumps, and his sales went through the roof. For several years in a row in the 1990s, he was voted not just the bestselling children's author in the country, but the bestselling author. He has written more than three hundred books and sold more than four hundred million copies. He lives in New York City with his wife, Jane, and his dog, Minnie. His son, Matthew, is a musician, sound designer, and composer.

· HEATHER GRAHAM ·

*N*ew York Times and *USA Today* bestselling author Heather Graham was born somewhere in Europe and kidnapped by gypsies when she was a small child. She went on to join the Romanian circus as a trapeze artist and lion tamer. When the circus came to South Florida, she stayed, discovering that she preferred to be a shark and gator trainer.

Not really.

Heather is the child of Scottish and Irish immigrants who met and married in Chicago, and moved to South Florida, where she has spent her life. (She has, at least, been to the Russian circus in Moscow, where she wished she was one of the incredibly talented and coordinated trapeze artists.) She has written over one hundred and fifty novels and novellas, has been published in approximately twenty-five languages, and has over seventy-five million books in print. Recent titles include *Nightwalker*, *Dust to Dust*, and *Unhallowed Ground*.

· · ·

· SUZANNE WEYN ·

S uzanne Weyn grew up in Williston Park, Long Island, New York. As a girl she was very interested in theater and in reading. Louisa May Alcott was her favorite author, but she also read every Sherlock Holmes story. She now lives in upper New York State in a 1930s cottage on a horse farm. She was graduated from the State University of New York at Binghamton and received her master's degree from Pace University.

Suzanne's recent novels include *The Bar Code Tattoo* (2004) and its sequel, *The Bar Code Rebellion* (2006). *The Bar Code Tattoo* was selected by the American Library Association (ALA) as an '05 Quick Pick for Reluctant Young Adult Readers and was an '07 Nevada Library nominee for Best Young Adult Fiction.

Her mystical, historic romance, *Reincarnation*, came out in January 2008 from Scholastic, and her novel, the bestselling *Distant Waves: A Novel of the Titanic*, was published in 2009. Her newest novel, *Empty*, came out in September 2010.

· JENNIFER ALLISON ·

J ennifer Allison's "The Perfects" was inspired in part by an old Victorian house the author passed each morning on her way to school in her small Michigan hometown. The author's favorite childhood memories include sharing spooky urban legends and ghost stories with friends while sitting up in a barn hayloft or around a campfire. "Part of the fun of being scared by a story was sharing that feeling with my friends and bonding with them through that experience. People respond to horror fiction very physically; maybe that's why the frightening tales always stuck in my memory." After working as a book editor, news reporter, and high school English teacher, Jennifer Allison rediscovered her childhood passion for stories that are both spooky and funny. She writes a series of novels about a teenage sleuth named Gilda Joyce—a much-loved character among young readers. Books in the *Gilda Joyce: Psychic Investigator* series have received starred reviews and a nomination for the Edgar Award.

▾ HEATHER BREWER ▾

Heather Brewer was not your typical teen growing up, and she's certainly not your typical adult now. She's a huge fan of the macabre, and when she's not reading horror, she's writing it. Heather completely blames her father for her warped mind, as she recalls fondly watching *The Twilight Zone* as a young child, as well as every cheesy horror film you can imagine. Heather is the author of the *New York Times* bestselling *The Chronicles of Vladimir Tod* series, as well as the upcoming Slayer Journals series and Bloodbound series. She doesn't believe in happy endings . . . unless they involve blood. She lives in Missouri with her husband and two children. Visit Heather at www.heatherbrewer.com.

PEG KEHRET

Peg Kehret's middle-grade books have won dozens of state young reader awards, as well as the PEN Center West Award in Children's Literature, the Golden Kite Award from the Society of Children's Book Writers and Illustrators, and the ASPCA's Henry Bergh Award. Her thriller, *Abduction!*, was nominated for an Edgar Award by the Mystery Writers of America.

She enjoys writing thrillers because she gets so many letters from readers who tell her, "I love scary books!"

Peg has two grown children and four grandchildren. She volunteers with animal welfare groups, and has included dogs, cats, llamas, elephants, bears, horses, and monkeys in her books. Three of her books are co-authored by Pete the Cat, who now gets fan mail of his own. Peg lives in Wilkeson, Washington, with her dog and two cats, all rescued animals. *Ghost Dog Secrets* was published in 2010 by Dutton Children's Books.

ALANE FERGUSON

People fascinate me—why do they do what they do, and how do their life experiences impact their choices? Since my best friend, Savannah, was the victim of a serial killer, I've spent a lot of my time studying the minds of murderers. I do believe in evil, but I also believe that *every* person is valuable, and I enjoy individuality—all are welcome at my table.

"Because of Savannah I began to write, winning the Edgar Allan Poe Award for my first novel. And, although I've published in other genres, the theme of mortality is a constant draw. In my YA Sleuth Forensic Mystery series, Cameryn, who works for her coroner father, sees death medically. Currently I'm expanding 'Dragonfly Eyes' into a novel that will explore the idea of justice and falling in love on the 'other side.' Through my family and my thirty-plus books I've learned to embrace life. Because you really never know . . ."

˙ RYAN BROWN ˙

As an actor Ryan Brown has held contract roles on *The Young and the Restless* and *Guiding Light*. He has also appeared on *Law & Order: SVU*, and starred in two feature films for Lifetime Television. His first novel, *Play Dead*, a comic supernatural thriller, was published in May of 2010. Ryan lives in New York with his wife and son.

˙ F. PAUL WILSON ˙

F. Paul Wilson is the award-winning, bestselling author of forty books and numerous short stories spanning science fiction, horror, adventure, medical thrillers, and virtually everything between. His work has appeared on the *New York*

Times and other bestseller lists. His novel *The Keep* was made into a perfectly awful film, and *The Tomb* is presently in development hell in Hollywood. He's perhaps best known for his urban mercenary character, Repairman Jack; he's written about Jack as an adult and most recently as a teen in *Jack: Secret Histories* and *Jack: Secret Circles.*

His work has been translated into twenty-four languages. He also has written for the stage, screen, and interactive media. He has won the Stoker Award, the Inkpot Award, the Porgie Award, and multiple Prometheus Awards. He was voted Grand Master by the World Horror Convention and received the Lifetime Achievement Award from the Horror Writers of America. He is listed in the fiftieth anniversary edition of *Who's Who in America.*

Paul resides at the Jersey shore and can be found on the web at www.repairmanjack.com.

ᐧ MEG CABOT ᐧ

*M*eg Cabot (her last name rhymes with *habit*—as in, "her books are habit-forming") is the #1 *New York Times* bestselling author of over twenty-five series and books for both adults and tweens/teens, selling over fifteen million copies worldwide.

Her Princess Diaries series, which is currently being published in over thirty-eight countries, was made into two hit movies by Disney. Meg also wrote the bestselling paranormal series The Mediator as well as the 1-800-Where-R-You? series (on which the television series *Missing* was based).

Meg is currently writing an edgy new YA series Airhead, as well as the Heather Wells mystery series for adult readers. Her new adult paranormal, *Insatiable*, was just released.

Meg divides her time between Key West, Indiana, and New York City, with a primary cat (one-eyed Henrietta), various backup cats, and her husband.

ᐧ WALTER SORRELLS ᐧ

Edgar Award–winner Walter Sorrells is the author of around thirty mystery and thriller novels, including books written both for young people and for adults.

Walter's most recent book for young adults is *Whiteout*, the third in his Hunted series.

A devoted martial artist, Walter holds a third-degree black belt in karate, and has also studied Brazilian Jujitsu, aikido, tai chi, and various Japanese sword arts. Walter is also a part-time swordsmith who specializes in hand forging Japanese-style swords and knives. He lives in Atlanta with his wife, Patti, and son, Jake (who is a heck of a baseball player). Someday Walter wants to write a book about the fun and insanity of youth baseball . . . but he hasn't gotten around to it yet!

■ ■ ■

· JAMES ROLLINS ·

James Rollins is the *New York Times* bestselling author of adventure thrillers, sold to over thirty countries. As a veterinarian, he still does volunteer work, but you'll often find him underground or underwater as an avid caver and scuba diver. These hobbies have helped in the creation of his earlier books, including *Subterranean*, *Deep Fathom*, and *Amazonia*.

His current Sigma series, starting with *Map of Bones*, has gone on to earn national accolades, such as one of 2005's "top crowd pleasers (*New York Times*) and as one of 2006's "hottest summer reads" (*People* magazine). His latest Sigma novel, titled *The Doomsday Key*, hit bestseller lists around the world in summer 2009, and in winter 2009, he introduced another of his standalone novels, *Altar of Eden*, featuring for the first time a veterinarian in the lead role.

If that wasn't enough, he has also completed the first of a middle-school series entitled *Jake Ransom and the Skull King's Shadow*, which debuted in April 2009, and the sequel, *Jake Ransom and the Howling Sphinx*, followed in April 2010.

And yes, sometimes he does come up for air.

· TIM MALEENY ·

Tim Maleeny is the award-winning author of several mystery novels for adult readers, including the critically acclaimed Cape Weathers Investigations series. *Stealing the Dragon*, his debut novel about a deadly female assassin, has been optioned for film. His comedic thriller *Jump* was called "hilarious" by the *Boston Globe,* and "a perfectly blended cocktail of escapism" by *Publishers Weekly.* He has won the prestigious Macavity Award for Best Short Story of the Year and also the Lefty Award for Best Humorous Mystery Novel.

"Ray Gun" is Tim's first story for young adults but is only the beginning. He is currently hard at work finishing a novel for young readers. You can find him online at www.timmaleeny.com.